Whiskey, Tango, Foxtrot? Over.
Keepin' It Real in Esoteric Magic

# Whiskey, Tango, Foxtrot? Over
# Keepin' It Real in Esoteric Magic

## Collen A'Miketh

Megalithica Books

Stafford, England

**Whiskey, Tango, Foxtrot? Over: Keepin' It Real in Esoteric Magic**
Collen A'Miketh
© 2009 First edition

All rights reserved, including the right to reproduce this book, or portions thereof, in any form.

The right of Collen A'Miketh to be identified as the author of this work has been asserted by them in accordance with the Copyright, Designs and Patents Act, 1988.

Cover Art: Collen A'Miketh and Andy Bigwood
Cover Design: Andy Bigwood
Editor: Taylor Ellwood
Layout: Taylor Ellwood

Set in Book Antiqua and Poor Richard

Megalithica Books Edition 2009

MB0130

A Megalithica Books Publication
http://www.immanion-press.com
info@immanion-press.com

8 Rowley Grove
Stafford ST17 9BJ
UK

ISBN 978-1-905713-30-1

# Acknowledgements

Many people made this book possible. I can't possibly name them all, so I'll stick to a select few. I can't express enough thanks for my wife, for Scarlett, my editors, or for Immanion Press.

# Table of Contents

| | |
|---|---|
| Foreword by Taylor Ellwood | 6 |
| Introduction | 8 |
| Boot Camp Basics | 11 |
| Tower Mage and Travelling Mage | 25 |
| It's Just a Theory | 49 |
| Ruh-Roh, Raggy | 61 |
| Back to Mystery School | 68 |
| Archetype Schmarkytype | 75 |
| Principia Pokera | 83 |
| The Obligatory Grimoire | 87 |
| A'Miketh's Memoir | 122 |
| Bibliography | 129 |

# Foreword by Taylor Ellwood

*Whiskey, Tango, Foxtrot? Over* is one of those books which at times will make you laugh and at other times do a double take as you say to yourself, "He wrote what?" Overall, however, what this book will really do is show you how not to take yourself or your magical practice so seriously that you forget the importance of keeping an open mind and being willing to learn. And that attitude, more than ever, is needed in occult practices.

In this book, Collen not only provides examples from his own life on how to keep it real in esoteric practices, he also makes an extremely important point that most contemporary magicians have forgotten. If you are focused only on magic, then you really have no perspective for actually utilizing it. The true magician is a renaissance person, who explores a variety of disciplines and their practices in order to better understand how magic fits in with everything else in the world and consequently when and where it should be employed. The magician understand that just as the myth of the rugged individual is ultimately harmful, so too is the tendency for magicians to focus only on magic, creating an insular focus that often lacks the finer tuning that a broader perspective will bring.

This book will make you laugh. It will also challenge your understanding of magic and its place in the world, as well as your life. I think the best books do make you laugh even as they challenge you. It's with some pride that I'm pleased to say that this book is approved by the Guild of Experimental Magicians, and is representative of the quality that we believe is essential for occult works to have. This book offers a key to the evolution of magic, while at the same time returning to the roots of what makes magic worth practicing: Service to the community, as well service to the self; innovation and creativity, as well as acknowledging the debt to the past.

Sit down, and relax. You'll soon be laughing and learning with this excellent book by Collen A'Miketh.

# Introduction

I don't know about you, but when I started my magical career I wanted to be a wizard: a fireball-throwing, mean, and magical machine. I am a magician, but I can't throw fireballs, chain lightning, walls of water, or even the occasional cantrip. Magic has become something else to me and it took me a while to define just exactly what that was and then put it to good use.

My need for magic as pyrotechnics quickly faded, but I later reached the point where I felt that I should have attained some higher level. That sense of mastery was missing. It was difficult for me to put my finger on what I needed. Frustration and the repeated banging of my noggin on my altar characterized my struggle to find answers. In spite of my aching head and surly disposition I continued casting about for something that might help me beyond the plateau on which my practice was stranded.

As I taught online classes, intensified my training, and did more research, I realized that I had the form down. I could do ritual and spell consistently and well. However, I still couldn't seem to figure out what came next. Eventually I realized that the next level was learning to choose to *act* in my life and not *react*. At first this answer didn't seem very magical, but it felt right. So I ran with it.

While running I happened to be carrying a copy of Henry Cornelius Agrippa's *Three Books of Occult Philosophy*. I tripped and dropped the book. It fell open to a page that said:

> "Whosoever therefore is desirous to study in this Faculty, if he be not skilled in naturall Philosophy... Mathematicks... [and] not learned in Theologie... he cannot be possibly able to understand the rationality of Magick. For there is no work that is done by meer Magick, nor any work that is meerly magical..."
> (Agrippa, 1651. p. 41)

Aha! There was more to magic then just magic. A magician needs to have other skills as well. Not only that, but work and magic were tied together. While thinking on this, I went to pick Agrippa's book off the floor and accidentally knocked *The Paradoxes of the Highest Science* by Eliphas Levi off of an inconveniently placed bookshelf. Quite serendipitously it opened to a chapter in which Levi opined:

> Moreover Magic must not be confounded with Magism. Magic is an occult force, and Magism is a doctrine which changes this force into a Power. A Magician without Magism is only a Sorcerer. A magist without magic is only one who KNOWS..." (Levi, 1922. p. 98)

and "

> ... To practise magic is to be a quack; to know magic is to be a sage..." (Levi, 1922. p.45)

Aha! Magic is a doctrine, something to live by. It's the use of magic as a doctrine that imbues it with power. While rubbing my tender knees, I reviewed my "Aha!" moments and took stock of how I *was* practicing magic as opposed to how I *wanted* to practice magic. I started to work on what magic might look like if I applied it every hour of every day... in and out, thick and thin, sober or drunk, er, sober at least. I realized that there was something to be said for using it as a *doctrine* and *philosophy*. Even better, when this doctrine was used side by side with the traditional techniques I'd spent years acquiring, there was a synergy that each type of approach lacked when used in isolation.

I now had the destination marked on my map, but no directions for how to get there. (This is the plateau I was referring to earlier, in case you were wondering.) Some schools tried to point the way with Theurgy, by having the magician use magic as a means for self-improvement. This moved towards the whole magic as philosophy idea, but never got overly chummy with the concept. Others went the Thaumaturgic route and hammered at external factors with spells to get results. This approach missed out completely on the philosophy stuff. Several went as far as asking me to list all my good and bad traits or having me attempt to identify who I was by looking at my personality in the context of the four Elements. But once those tasks were completed, my questions then became "Ok. Now what?" and "How do I fix the stuff that needs fixing?"

I realized the answer to those questions were that techniques like the Body of Light, not thinking, and controlled breathing could be used effectively outside the confines of the ritual chamber. In short, I could use those exercises to retrain myself to act instead of react. When I encountered a situation that invoked a conditioned response (like fight or flight), instead of

## Introduction

yielding, I could teach myself to invoke my magical exercises to override that response and do something differently.

This book provides an approach to applying magic in very mundane situations and in very mundane ways to achieve results that are... well... quite magical. I start the book with an overview of the magical techniques that can be used in the everyday and review them in the context of applying them mundanely. Each exercise includes an example of its traditional use. I then move to ideas and exercises that can be used in the real world. From there I offer a magical theory that gels well with this approach, then touch on the risks and rewards of magical practice. The next couple of chapters cover ideas that indirectly touch on everyday magic. I finish off with some war stories that cover my twenty years of magical practice and a short grimoire that provides some ideas you can use in your own practice.

I wrote this book with an intermediate practitioner in mind. I don't like talking down to people so I assume you have a couple years of experience and are acquainted with the ideas and concepts that aren't my own. Furthermore, I wrote this book as if I were talking to someone I took as my own apprentice. The tone is sometimes blunt, irreverent, crude, and lacking polish... but my wife informs me that it is a rather accurate portrayal of my personality.

Collen A'Miketh

# Chapter 1: Boot Camp Basics

Training ourselves in basic magical techniques is a burden when the skills acquired have no apparent application in every day activities. Acquiring and applying skills like sitting perfectly still or not thinking is difficult, but being able to do so has a profound impact on how we live our lives and practice our magic. In this chapter, I present a variety of techniques I've learned over the years and thoughts on how they can be used every day to modify and improve our habits, reactions and behaviors.

The ideas presented in this chapter are intended to be used as extensions of our normal magical exercise and can be utilized in tandem with our current practice. In other words, we can continue to practice the basics in the usual way (with the intent to train ourselves to do magic) and then learn to reapply those exercises in real world situations. They can be used to try and override our conditioned reactions to life's situations and instead take action. Though this book isn't intended as a 101 course, I've taken the liberty of giving examples for each exercise I present. Where appropriate, I detail some of my thoughts and experiences regarding the application of these exercises.

## Body of Light

Our first exercise is known to many traditions as the Body of Light. This "body" comes in many forms and different practitioners work with it in different ways. Some approach it as an Astral Body distinct from their usual body. Others use a process of imagining their real body bathed in light or radiating light. Some training systems use a combination of both techniques. Whichever method is employed, the development of this body is important. If we strip away the esoteric reasons usually given, like regulating our Astral energy patterns, we see that the Body of Light teaches us to concentrate, to enter a different mental state, and to heighten awareness of our physical body.

On the practical side of this exercise, we begin to unite body and mind into a cohesive whole. This is in direct contrast to traditions that consider body and mind separate entities. We can use this exercise to de-condition ourselves from the last umpteen hundred years of thought that insisted on dividing body and mind into matter and spirit and then flaying the poor unsuspecting matter part of the equation into some sort of submission. This de-conditioning is important because body and mind are linked. The Body of Light provides us with the basic skills to pay attention to our mind and our body simultaneously with respect and empathy. It lays a natural foundation for the exercises that follow and helps us begin our path out of the world of reaction and into the world of willed action.

Begin breathing slowly and regularly while your body is in a relaxed position. Next, as you breathe in, imagine that you are drawing light up into your body from the bottom of your spine and down into your body through the top of your head. Imagine that light slowly spreading to fill your body and your spine glowing as the light infuses your body. Once your body is filled with light, visualize your entire body glowing with light. As you breathe out, visualize the white light flowing outwards from your solar plexus with each breath. (Note: This is my personal variation of the Body of Light as taught by the Order of Bards, Ovates and Druids.)

## Breathing

The next exercise teaches us to focus on breathing. When we force ourselves to breathe in rhythmic patterns, we enhance our awareness of our physical state and begin the process of entering altered states of consciousness. Breath controls the body, which exerts a powerful control on the mind because the two are parts of the same whole. This provides the ability to alter our mental state and obtain some semblance of control over our physical reactions to stimuli.

When we get upset or excited we tend to breathe more rapidly (That good ol' fight or flight response which isn't always so good) and when we are relaxed or sleeping (or meditating like good magicians do) we breathe more slowly. This exercise forces our bodies to breathe in a non-habitual pattern, which can then be applied to help us align with a desired emotional state. Here, we are aligning with a feeling of meditative calm. We're also reinforcing the idea that we have control over our actions and ourselves. These exercises can be expanded upon to induce other states, too, though they are more useful when used to disrupt intense emotional patterns like anger, fear, and arousal. Whatever the application, we can use breathing exercises to OVERRIDE our natural reactions to stimuli and thereby use "magic" to create a willed, physical, premeditated *action* instead of *reacting* to a situation.

Become aware of your breathing and begin to breathe in a pattern of breathing in, holding it, breathing out, and holding it. Pick a count for each part of the pattern. Heartbeats are a good measuring stick. Use a balanced count, (i.e. Breathe in for a three count, hold for a three count, breathe out for a three count, hold for a three count) or a staggered count (i.e. Breathe in for a four count, hold for a three count, breathe out for a four count, hold for a three count). Pick the pattern that is comfortable for you.

Before continuing to the next exercise, let's address some of the challenges and finer points of breathing. Proper breathing is done from the diaphragm, not the chest. Basic singing courses teach this. In a nutshell, you inflate your chest and entire torso (stomach area included) and then breathe in and out without moving your chest to expel the air. If you don't breathe like this, and most folks don't, it's damned uncomfortable and takes practice to do consistently and correctly.

This brings us to the part of the exercise where we hold the breath in for a couple of counts. Holding in comes naturally to swimmers and pot smokers, so if you fall into either of those categories, feel free to steal that skill and apply it here. Sans the water and/or Mary Jane, of course.

Holding the breath out can also be difficult, particularly since it can engender feelings of suffocation. Ironically, it's done all the time in daily life. You just have to pay attention to when it happens and expand upon it. Have you ever been daydreaming and then remembered to breathe in? Or been in a suspenseful situation, and remembered to breathe in? Or, been so shocked you forgot to breathe? If you can become aware of these incidents you now have a handy crib for applying the skill in your breathing exercises. Alternately, you can go to a local swimming pool and sit on the bottom. The expelling of your air before going under pretty much teaches everything you need to know and gives you and your body the opportunity to overcome your rather justified aversion to not breathing in general.

We tackled our physical reactions to stimuli with breathing. The unification of body and mind continues by learning to still the mind and govern our mental and emotional reactions. These techniques are also quite useful as a final safeguard against a failed attempt to control a physical reaction using physical means, for example breathing. If the body has begun to react then we can use our mind to modify, control, disregard, or suck it up and drive right on through the physical reactions to stress.

Stilling the mind is usually learned in stages. It starts with observing our thoughts as our mind meanders in its usual fashion, then concentrating on a single train of thought, followed by focusing on a single idea, and finally not thinking of anything at all. Like breathing, we can use our "mind void" skill to override conditioned reactions to situations and stimuli. Once we do that we begin to exert Will in a manner of our choosing.

**Example**

Create a "Thought Sink" by lighting a candle, staring at a blank section of wall, black card or other item. When ready, use breathing to center yourself. "Centering" in this context, is used to describe a state of mind where you become clear and focused. Become aware of your thoughts. Let them run their course for a bit and then, as thoughts occur, imagine that they are sucked into the Thought Sink and eliminated. As you do this, imagine a continuous hum in your head that drowns all external sound. Once you become proficient at arresting your thoughts, you should find it possible to think of nothing at all by withdrawing your mind from any thought that arises.

In practice, "not thinking" is a difficult state to achieve for any length of time and the process is different for different practitioners. For me, it feels as if I'm physically pulling my mind away from thoughts. Then, at some point, I just stop thinking for short periods of time. Many times, I hold onto my not thinking state for as long as possible and then, as my thoughts again begin to intrude, I switch back to my Thought Sink. When I've regained my focus, I switch back to not thinking.

An interesting side effect of this alternating "single thought/not thinking" is that, if I do it long enough, I drop into a light trance state. This switch to a trance state is usually preceded by an odd "popping" sensation followed by the sense that I am asleep and awake at the same time. Or, I wake up about thirty minutes later rested and refreshed from my unscheduled nappy time. The reverse is also true. I've awakened from a nap in a light trance.

## Visualization

Assuming we have acquired some skill in the preceding exercises, we need to find ways to apply those skills proactively. This brings us to visualization techniques. These exercises include the common skill of vivid visualization, deeply feeling an emotion, and imagining a desired outcome to a situation. This skill can be fine tuned by first learning to hold a symbol in the mind's eye and then projecting it onto a wall. We can go further by visualizing a clock on a wall, hearing it tick, and smelling the dust that lies on the clock's mantel.

The ticking clock example comes from Bardon, Franz (2001) and may seem perversely detailed. The underlying concept is that visualization involves more than sight and is intended to engage all our senses. In fact, we can visualize with any of our five senses. Don't let the ocular nature of the term "visualize" limit the possibilities.

We each have at least one sense that lends itself easily to visualization and others that aren't as well developed. In the end, we want to enhance our ability to use all senses in visualization. We may not use them equally across the board, but, whenever possible, we want to be able to use them all. So, if you are weak in a particular area of visualization, take some time to develop it and make it a point to use it.

The purpose of visualization is self-hypnosis. We train ourselves to inject false stimuli into the information we receive. From now on, I refer to this incoming sensory data as "the Data Stream." I also refer to outgoing information as "the Data Stream." Visualization injects our chosen stimuli into the incoming Data Stream. Modify the Data Stream and we modify our reaction to the data. Modify our reaction and we change how we interact with the world. Change how we react to the world and the world sometimes changes with us. This is great and this is wonderful. This is what magic is all about! But, this is also where magic gets risky.

## Risky Magic – A Word About Reality

When we modify our Data Stream we are rejecting *Reality* in preference for our own *view of Reality* and we are "in control" of ourselves. However, we risk going too far and rendering ourselves incapable of receiving proper feedback from the world around us.

Utterly rejecting Reality for our own version thereof is madness. To avoid going God's Balls Batshit, our Data Stream modification must be rooted in Reality and must look to that Reality to ensure that we haven't completely lost touch. Our Reality touchstones include people's reactions to our actions or the results of natural law, like gravity. *Look Ma, I'm flying!!! Aaaiii..* Both can technically be ignored. ...*eeeee*... Both have repercussions for doing so. *SPLAT!*

The first two examples are consistently more difficult for me than the final exercise. My symbols have this uncanny ability to shimmer, morph, expand, contract, and flit about in ways that I don't want. I think that the final example is easier for me because I'm busy with more sensory data and it's easy to ignore my inaccuracies when I'm dealing with a lot of information. Those first two are pretty pure and there isn't enough fluff to hide what my mind is or isn't doing.

### Example 1

Select a simple symbol; this can be a geometric shape or an occult shape. If you prefer, prior to performing this exercise, draw this shape on a card or piece of paper. If you have drawn your symbol, look at it and then close your eyes. Otherwise, form the symbol in your mind and then close your eyes. Hold the symbol in your mind's eye as long as possible.

### Example 2

This is very similar to the preceding example, except in this exercise you open your eyes and project the image onto a blank surface. It can be a wall or something equally nondescript.

### Example 3

Pick a visualization that engages all senses. It must have an auditory, visual, tactile, and olfactory component to it. Using the clock example previously mentioned, the clock was the visual, the ticking was the auditory, tactile might be the feel of the clock casing, and olfactory was the smell of the dust on the clock. Other examples might be a pot of stew simmering on the stove or a car with its hood up and the engine idling.

Enter Code 4567 to enter
Confirmation number HM@D8425CR

Budget Travellers Deal 2B
235 77th Street #2B
North Bergen, NJ 07047
United States

Mike.ribeiro@live.ca

Also, let's connect on LinkedIn! Aside from the professional aspect, I have in keeping up with students and watching their careers blossom, graduates of this course will be invited to join an alumni group for graduates of this course.

## Data Stream (or Sensory) Exercises

At this point, we must consider what the Data Stream is and how to properly use it. To address those questions, we look to exercises intended to highlight each of our five senses. They include looking for a particular color or focusing attention on everything we hear. Some want us to go for a walk and experience colors, sounds, smells and tactile sensations while avoiding the verbal dialogue we invariably use to categorize the incoming information. These exercises are sometimes extended to paying attention to all nonverbal data coming from another person, animal or plant.

These exercises are used to enhance and filter awareness. There is a lot of information in the Data Stream and filters keep it manageable. We can't possibly deal with all of it. But as magicians, we strive to expand what we can work with. As we extend our abilities, the initial influx of new information can be as bewildering as having no information to work with at all. Sensory exercises help by showing us where our filters are and how to use them well. Once we know where they are and how they work, we can begin to modify them so we get what we need from our Data Stream without drowning in it. We learn to be better information swimmers.

These exercises begin by teaching you to become aware of the data streaming into your senses. Next, they help you to maintain that awareness without using words to categorize or modify it. Finally, you can continue to use these exercises to enhance your ability to receive information.

When I put these exercises into practice, I generally find myself in one of two situations: practicing in a new environment and practicing in a familiar environment. In a new environment it is easier for me to grab lots of information and miss the minutia. In a familiar environment, I tend to have a grip on the details but, because I'm not in sensory overdrive, I fight with myself to look at the same boring old things to glean more information.

### Example 1

Go for a walk and note colors, sounds, smells, and objects. Make a conscious effort to uncouple your verbal mind from the incoming data. Avoid verbally labeling what you experience. Focus on one sense at a time and then try applying the same level of attention to all senses at once.

### Example 2

Make a concerted effort to see, hear, taste, smell, and otherwise understand all the data another person is sending to you. This information can include posture, scents, inflections, mannerisms, words chosen during speech, and the person's apparent taste in cars, clothes, and music. Do not try to judge or categorize the information; just acquire as much information as you can. You can also try doing this with a plant, animal, rock, insect, or even yourself.

### Perspective Exercises

We expand on the sensory exercises by adding perspective. Perspective training comes in many forms, but I like to break them into two classes, the "direct" and the "indirect." The direct methods are probably already familiar. They generally have us enter an altered state of consciousness, usually via meditation, and then ask us to think about a particular subject from a different point of view. In a practical sense these are applied in everyday life by encouraging us to see things in ways we normally don't consider. By shifting viewpoints we broaden the information from the Data Stream. Like the preceding sensory exercises, perspective teaches us about our filters and how they work.

Magical symbol systems, such as runes, utilize the indirect perspective. When we memorize a symbol system we give ourselves an indirect path to altering perspective. First, we alter our perspective by structuring it in terms of a symbol. The symbol functions as a mediator, or filter, between Reality and ourselves. When we use the symbol as a signifier, we highlight certain qualities associated with the chosen representation (that would be the symbol there, Big Kahuna). Next, we interact with it and use it to limit or expand the data with which we work.

Think of this limiting or expanding of the data as placing a picture frame around the information we want to work with. This separates it from the other information in the Data Stream. Once we've created this frame, or symbol, we can focus on the information inside the frame, outside the frame or the frame itself. When we focus on the frame itself the frame becomes a symbol that represents everything within the frame.

The level of abstraction in these exercises gets us closer to (or is it farther from?) the frame that creates our perspective by boxing in portions of the Data Stream and presenting us with a filtered view, like looking through the picture frame. As we step back from the frame, or artificially construct one, it becomes easier to highlight, isolate, and work with parts of the Data Stream from different points of view. This type of work reinforces the magical thinking paradigm, which assumes the interconnected nature of things by finding wildly different but somehow associated ways of working with information.

### Example - The Fencepost

Find a fencepost and use it as a focus for meditation. Think of the fencepost from the perspective of a bird, a termite, ant, and bee. Consider how it looks when viewed from the air and from the side opposite from where you sit (or stand). Think of how it appears to an earthworm.

What does the fencepost think it is?
What does grass think a fencepost is?
If the fencepost were a person, what kind of person would it be?
How would it talk to you?

### Example - Symbol View

Select a rune or symbol from your chosen magical alphabet (for initial work, start with a positive one). Spend an entire day viewing life in the context of the meaning of the rune or symbol.

### Example - Variations on a Theme

Spend two hours experiencing life from the vantage of the color blue, then yellow. Next, spend two hours and alternate between love and apathy. Next, experience life from the perspective of a spell and then experience life from the perspective of just getting things done the mundane way.

## Self-Control

Self-control exercises are the building blocks for conscientious living. They teach us to pay attention to our speech, what we think, and how we feel and act. By paying attention to these things, we inculcate in ourselves the ability to do something about them. Speech exercises deal with the mechanics of paying attention to what passes our lips. Words have power. Thought exercises focus on identifying the root cause of a particular line of thought. They also teach us how to think through an intended course of action and divine its consequences. Exercises focused on our feelings provide a means to examine and integrate emotions. They encourage us to ask the "Who, What, How, When, and Why?" questions that give us insight into why we react a certain way. The end result is the ability to choose our action. We learn to be patient until the proper time, or act immediately when a course of action presents itself.

These exercises help us monitor our speech, thoughts, feelings, and actions. The speech exercises, when practiced, tend to inject pauses into our speech patterns. Sometimes we come across as thoughtful and measured, sometimes we sound like idiots. The thought exercises take time and discipline, first to remember to do them and then to actually do them. The same goes for the feeling exercises, though for different reasons. It's understandably difficult to remember to do the feeling exercises during highly charged emotional situations or shortly afterwards. Reviewing our feelings at the end of the day is perfectly acceptable. The action exercises can be done real time or after the fact, in your head. In fact, it may be more appropriate to do the second action exercise at a later time. Acting first in real life may have unintended consequences. * DOH *.

## Examples – Speech

Eliminate a word from your vocabulary. This word does have to be a word you use everyday, but there are no restrictions otherwise. Note that this technique is found in many training systems. Chaos Magic, Qabalism, Golden Dawn, and Thelema come to mind.

Ask yourself if what you say is true and constructive. Do not speak it if it does not meet those criteria. There is an Eastern proverb for this from Sri Sathya Sai Baba (n.d.) and it goes something like "Before you speak, think - Is it necessary? Is it true? Is it kind? Will it hurt anyone? Will it improve on the silence?"

### Examples - Thoughts

Review your thought patterns at least twice a day. Make notes as to what you think about and how long you think about it. Attempt to identify the source of each particular thought. In other words, if you are thinking about eating, ask yourself if you are hungry. If you are thinking about work, ask yourself, "Am I upset about work? What made me upset? Is there something deeper than X happening that made me upset? Why?" and so on. The deeper you can go, the more effective this exercise is.

For a day, ask yourself the following questions: Is what I am thinking true? Is it only true for me?

### Examples – Feeling

When a strong emotion surfaces ask yourself "Who, What, Where, How, When and Why?" Get to the root cause of what you are feeling, if possible. You can do this at the time, or later in review. Try to do it at the time, if possible.

After feeling a strong emotion, personify it in meditation. Sit down and talk to him/her. Ask questions that help you to understand the emotion. See if the conversation can help you find the best way to integrate the emotion.

### Examples - Actions

For an hour or two, hold off on taking a course of action and think about it in depth before proceeding. Analyze your motives and the potential outcome, and then act. If possible, make it a point to double the information you have regarding a particular situation before you act.

Act first, question second. For an hour or two, act on the information you have without waiting for more information. Is this easier or more difficult than waiting?

## Affirmations

The Affirmation is a useful magical tool with several different applications. Some traditions chant "power words" or phrases, like AUM, over and over again. If done properly, it teaches us to hold on to a particular thought throughout the day. With it we learn that, by extension, we can hold on to particular mental and emotional states at will. Once we do that, we can then shift those states according to our Will and pleasure, and not necessarily the dictates of the world around us.

The other form of the Affirmation is used to help us to believe we can accomplish something or be a particular kind of person. We bring about personal change by repeating to ourselves the qualities we want to develop or goals we want to achieve. If this affirmation teaches anything, it teaches that self-modification works and we can alter our selves by altering what we think about, tell ourselves, and focus on during our day. (For better or worse.)

I don't give an example of the first type of Affirmation. There is plenty of material out there that covers the subject more succinctly and accurately than I can. If you're interested, excellent examples of this can be found in Crowley's *Book 4* (2004).

### Example

The second form of the affirmation is something we repeat daily to ourselves. It is highly personal. It can be a single statement or a conglomeration of statements constructed under the following rules:

Never write the Affirmation down. Ever. People change. Having the Affirmation reside in your head makes it a living thing that slowly evolves over time and exists only in.... (say the next two words in a big ballsy announcer voice) The Present (I knew you could). If you can't refer back to it, you are not hamstrung by worrying about living up to an Affirmation you used a year ago. Furthermore, by never writing it down you *make* yourself remember what you are trying to accomplish. Say it at least four days a week, but never all seven. This takes the conscious mind out of the loop and gives the Affirmation a chance to trickle into your subconscious and do its thing. These affirmations are ALWAYS in the affirmative and you can change them as you progress, grow, and/or identify areas that need improvement. Speak them aloud, if possible, but speak them while you are alone. This final rule ensures that you are the final arbiter of who you want to be. When these kinds of things are shared with others, your ideas become subject to what those folks want you to be (or already perceive you as being). The speaking aloud bit means that you are physically *doing something* (even though this is technically symbolic) instead of just thinking about it.

## Examples

Good – I have a photographic memory.
Not Good – I don't forget things.
Good – I am disciplined. I am honorable. I am a wizard.
Not Good – I don't lie. I'm not mundane.
Good – I am my ideal weight.
Not Good – I don't overeat.

## Spell Casting

Spell casting can also be approached as magical exercise. In this context we focus on the spell as a means to an end and not the end itself. To be successful with this we have to consider the act of spell casting as having two stages of practice and not one. The first stage is comprised of our exercises. These exercises teach us *how* to practice. They are the building blocks of spell casting and contain trance, visualization, and ritualistic skills. Our daily exercises are akin to what a sport professional does to hone their skill set prior to the big game.

The second stage of practice is the spell. This stage is the symbolic representation of what we'd like to do in the real world. This is practicing the form we want our Will to take, which we do by using the basic skills we've been developing in the first stage. Using the sports analogy, this is the practice game a player participates in to incorporate the basic skills they've been working on and learn to use them together cohesively during the game. The *real magic*, the manifesting of Will, happens when we walk out of our ritual chamber and *do something* about what we've been practicing. It's the difference between talk and action. It's game day.

## Some Final Thoughts

In closing, to properly apply these exercises we must find ways to push, pull or drag our magical practice into the everyday. Try holding a single thought in the hurly-burly of the local mega-mart, or doing the Body of Light while you type at work. Imagine a clock hovering over someone's head during a meeting or while at the gas station. See if you can give yourself a different physiological reaction to a typical fight or flight situation (like arguing with your spouse, or maybe meeting someone at work you don't like).

It's not easy. It took me a good six months from realizing that I had the ability to *act* instead of *react* before I was achieving some success at overcoming a lifetime of habitual response. Even then, my success rate was less than stellar. In fact, it was abysmal. I kept at it. I figured if I could see and hear a paisley clad monk banging a gong at the end of the hall at work, then I had the control to act instead of react. It was overcoming years of habit that was difficult. And it still is. When you are finally to a point where you are acting instead of reacting, you've moved your practice out of what I like to call "The Tower" and into your life. This is a good thing.

# Chapter Two: Tower Mage and Traveling Mage

Anyone who has been around the altar a couple of times knows that magic isn't worth much if it can't be applied in the real world. Sure, a spell let Reality know what form I wanted my Will to take, but once outside my ritual chamber I was faced with the reality of the world as it was. And what I wanted was sometimes at very ugly odds with the way things were. I realized that my personal course in advanced magic consisted of trying to get daily life up to par with what I felt it should be for a magician. It was also about making my daily life as well-kept as my magical life. The true test of being a magician wasn't casting the circle; *it was taking the circle with me,* and acting according to magical principles all the time.

The more I thought about this the more I considered how exactly I went about everyday magic. I looked at what it felt like and how I acted when practicing it. I took notes on my magical effectiveness when I was out and about. As I assessed my state of magical affairs I came to the conclusion that I'd figured out that I could shape my world to some degree, and I wasn't doing it by ignoring Reality and insisting that "It's my way, or the highway!" My practice was a very give-and-take relationship with the world around me.

I thought of it in these terms: People comfortable and familiar with their jobs are generally good at what they do. At some point, they no longer need a book or large quantities of instruction to get from point A to point B. They have been trained, or trained themselves, to perform the required tasks. They also have a subset of skills which, when required by circumstances, allow them to learn new things and implement what they've learned. Magic is no different. Reading a single book or going to a three day course does not a magician make. Time, effort, practice, mistakes (lots of those!), and finding new ways to do things all go into making a magician.

To make this division between stylized ritual practice and daily living, I use the terms Traveling Magic and Tower Magic. When I say Tower or Tower Magic, it's my short hand way of indicating magic practiced in isolation from the real world. It's what we usually think of when we think of practicing magic. It includes activities like meditation, spell casting, and ritual. In the Tower we learn discipline, new ways to think, new ways to act, and new ways to manifest Will. In the Tower we train ourselves to implement those things.

Traveling Magic (or Traveling), on the other hand, is what we do in every day life. It's taking the practice we've been doing in private and finding ways to make it work every day. Peter Carroll calls it "Open Hand Magic." I forget what the Chinese call it. I probably couldn't pronounce it correctly anyways. That being said, Traveling Magic is inextricably linked with Tower Magic. When we travel the intent isn't to "do magic." It's to live magically.

If we aren't careful, it is possible that this intent to live magically can get lost in our desire to perform magic. The Golden Dawn magician Israel Regardie (2001) suggested that after a certain stage, some of the training exercises weren't supposed to be done every day... if ever again. Once we learn to walk, we walk instead of hobbling ourselves by continuing to crawl.

Like lots of skills and learning, the process of being a day-to-day magician starts in the safety of "the Tower." The Tower is a safe haven to come to terms with who we are now and who we want to be in the future. It's much better to do this in the Tower. Dealing with our shortcomings is never a fun process. I'd much rather drag them out and look at them alone. I tend to get cranky when my limitations slap me in the face in public.

## Tools to Build Tools

In the computer world there is an operating system called Unix. I once read that Unix was powerful because it was a collection of tools designed to help us build more tools. I always took that to mean that there was this bunch of utilities we could string together to do complex tasks. Boot Camp Basics presented the equivalent of the utilities. In this chapter, we move on to more complex tasks that have some of those simple exercises in them.

The difference between Unix and magical exercise is that, in Unix, if we miss a needed piece then stuff doesn't work right. In both Unix and magic, things often work, but we usually don't have a good grasp on the hows or whys. Without a good understanding of the fundamentals, we don't have the tools to properly troubleshoot the problem or improve upon our magical practice. When something goes wrong and we get unexpected or unintended results in either area, we may find ourselves saying, "It should not be doing that!"

To help remedy this, you can use the basic exercises to help define the major characteristics of a complex working and then use them as signposts for our magical troubleshooting. Magical complexity tends to defy full categorization, so it is good to keep this in mind as we work to understand what we are doing.

To help clarify the inner workings of this chapter's examples, I indicate which Boot Camp exercises are being used. This isn't a completely accurate portrayal of what is going on, but does give some insight into the inner workings and may give you some ideas for creating complex routines on your own. It may also give you some ideas on how to break down other complex occult tasks to achieve a better understanding of how they work.

## Collateral Change

Dragging my magic out of the Tower and Traveling with it wasn't easy. In practice, Tower Magic pointed out my flaws, but I could never seem to fix the damn things completely. It was very discouraging. And yet, as I struggled, I found a phenomenon I called *Collateral Change*. I began to use this term to describe the side effects of trying to learn a new habit or skill. Sometimes as we struggle to make ourselves better we don't really fix the problem identified, but we do get better at dealing with life in general and with situations that engage the same root habit or skill we are trying to learn (or unlearn).

For example, I can't seem to keep my mouth shut in situations where I feel wronged or where I am surprised (for good or ill). Even after I identified this, I wasn't able to properly address the issue. But, as I kept working, I realized that I was holding my tongue more often than I used to in some situations. Being surprised or feeling threatened are still stumbling blocks to acting appropriately, but I don't fall quite as frequently or quite as hard. In short, I now have the ability to recognize that I'm digging a hole and put the shovel down.

This example of Collateral Change showed me that my Tower Magic was becoming easier to take with me when I traveled out my front door. I found that basic magical exercises, which on the surface seemed to have little or no relation to interacting with daily life, were paying off by becoming the focal point for self-discipline and eventually becoming habit. The more I looked, the more Collateral Change I found.

As I reviewed what I was doing and the impact of Collateral Change, I realized that my Tower Magic, whether meditation or spell, was about shaping and reshaping myself to act and respond in the ways I intended. It occurred to me that spell casting was about fostering awareness, discipline, and results, *in that order*. The order is important because we need to be aware of something that needs changing and disciplined enough to do something about it. Because my Traveling Magic was results-oriented instead of ritual-oriented it meant that the only thing I needed to do magic was myself.

Real magic isn't about wearing a robe to work and thumping around the corridors of Corporate America with a staff. That's about as useful as trying to shove wet spaghetti up a wild cat's ass. Being magically productive isn't easy either; we must spend a fair amount of time in our Tower forming cornerstones for living our magical life in the real world. The discussions that follow take the Boot Camp Basics we discussed in the previous chapter and discuss ways they might be implemented in daily life. Some may come easily; others may be difficult. But, because Collateral Change is a good thing, the important part is to start Traveling with our magic. Oh, and to be quite truthful, I don't take my staff to work because I'd beat somebody with it. I imagine it would be immensely therapeutic, but counterproductive.

Collateral Change is a result of magical practice and doesn't directly map to any Boot Camp exercises. I suppose I could make the case that to become aware of this change we use a combination of the Sense/Data Stream exercises in the context of paying attention, the Perspective exercises to step outside of our daily routine long enough to observe the extent of the change, and Self-Control to continue to apply what we've learned. We can also make an Affirmation out of our success to help us feel that doing the occult thing is getting worthwhile results.

## Memorization

With the notable exception of the Golden Dawn and derivative schools, modern magical practice downplays or ignores memorization. It is unfortunate that it gets short shrift. Memorization mentally embeds symbols, words, and phrases in ways that change our perceptions of Reality. Once we've crammed those concepts into our noggins, the mind is, at least to that small extent, transformed. We've heard the maxim before, "change your mind and change the world." On another level, Traveling Magic isn't possible if we can't call symbols and spells to mind at will. Memorization can also be used to perform full rituals without stopping to read the instructions. This can be expanded upon to perform full rituals in the mind, which is an important tool in the Traveling magician's toolbox. My personal experience has been that full-blown rituals performed in the theatre of my mind are just as effective as rituals performed in the real world.

In a small attempt to redress the marginalization of memory, I'd like to present a short set of exercises and ideas for learning how to memorize things. These are very basic, yet we can use them to great effect in our magical practice. For example: The techniques presented for memorizing lists can be applied to learning magical alphabets or other sets of symbols, like the four Elements and their associations or the twelve Signs of the Zodiac. The cipher technique can be used to memorize a full ritual. I wish I could say I came up with these ideas. The list and number memorization techniques are derived from a series of pamphlets by Welham Clark (circa 1920). I believe I have the only extant copy of the originals. The cipher technique is derived from Freemasonry.

### How to Memorize a List

To remember a list of things, link the pieces of information together using the rules below. Repeat the process several times, connecting each item in turn. Use vivid sensory images that have a lot of power in your mind. By using your five senses to add depth to a link between two ideas (or even to add depth and imagery the ideas themselves) you create a "hook," which makes it easier to recall the information. When you have the list memorized, move on to something else. Return to your list after five minutes, ten minutes, thirty minutes, an hour, and then at the end of the day.

### Rules for Linking Ideas

* There must be *two* and *only two* ideas associated at once, no matter what the length or number of items in the series.
* The only way to recall the series is link by link. The first idea *must* bring to mind the second *only*, the second *only the third*, and so on.

* Make a vivid association between each pair of ideas. Use as many of your five senses as you can when associating ideas to intensify the link.

**Exercise**

Memorize the following list:

| | |
|---|---|
| Colonel | Army |
| Army | Cannon |
| Cannon | Noise |
| Noise | Thunder |
| Thunder | Lightning |
| Lightning | Light |
| Light | Black |
| Black | Ink |
| Ink | Pen |
| Pen | Hand |
| Hand | Head |
| Head | Skull |
| Skull | Ghost |
| Ghost | Terror |

The key is to link colonel to Army. Then link Army to Cannon and Cannon to Noise. Your linking process might be something like: "A colonel is in the Army. The Army has cannons. Cannons make noise. A noisy noise is thunder. Thunder and Lightning. (Very, very frightening!) Lightning is light. Light's opposite is black. Black is the color of ink. Ink goes in a pen. A pen is held in the hand. I hold my hand up to my head. A head is a skull. Skulls remind me of ghosts. Ghosts inspire terror."

Try it. Right now. You might be surprised at how well you can remember this. In fact, I'm willing to bet if you can remember it forwards you can also remember it backwards just as easily! Once you are done with that, pick your favorite magical alphabet, Tarot deck or occult symbol set, put on your Mentat hat and get cracking!

**Memorizing Numbers**

To memorize numbers, dates and the like, associate numbers with letters and make words out of the letters. Using the chart, the process is pretty straightforward. This system assumes the *phonetic* equivalent of the letters and does not represent each letter. For example, "hill" stands for one and not eleven because the "L" is a single sound. "Lily," on the other hand, stands for eleven because there are two "L" sounds.

*Number Association Chart*

| | | 0 | | |
|---|---|---|---|---|
| | | C as in Cipher | | |
| | | S as in Sign | | |
| | | Z as in Zero | | |
| | 1 | | 2 | |
| | L | | N | |
| 3 | | 4 | | 5 |
| M | | R | | F or V |
| 6 | 7 | 8 | | 9 |
| SH as in Shop | | K/C as in Cow/King | | P or B |
| J/G as in James/George | | G/Q as in God/Queen | | |
| CH as in Charles | D or T | NG as in Ring | | |
| DGE/TCH as in Watch, Wedge and Assure | | X as in Express | | |

## Using the Chart

1 = L. This is easy to remember because a lowercase L is a single straight line, resembling the number 1.

2 = N. N is substituted for 2 because it combines 2 upright strokes.

3 = M. When turned on its side, 3 looks like an M.

4 = R. The word "four" has 4 letters in it and the last letter of "four" is R.

5 = F or V. F and V appear in the word "five." 5 also represents phonetic F sounds such as of the PH in "photo" and the GH in "cough."

6 = SH, soft J/G and CH. SH as in "shop," J as in James, G as in "George" and CH as in "Charles." The numeral 6 also represents phonetic J/G sounds such as the DGE in "wedge" and the phonetic TCH in "watch."

7 = D or T. If you cut off the right part of the T, it looks like a 7. D is close to T in its consonant sound.

8 = Hard C, G, K, QU, X and NG. The sound of C as in "cow," G as in "God," K as in "king," and QU as in "queen," X as in "example" and NG as in "ring."

9 = P or B. P looks like 9 reversed and B has a similar sound.

0 = S, soft C, and Z. These sounds are found in both cipher and zero.

AEIOUHWY are the only "free" letters without numeric values.

A mnemonic designed by Scarlett Sankey (personal conversation 2008) might help:

**One** is the Loneliest number.
but **two** Nuns
Met **three** MadMen who gave
**Four** Red Rats
**Five** FaVors and
waTCHed James, George, and Charles weDGe **six** SHorts and
Drink DieT **seven** up as
the Cow God Gave **eight** riNGs to the eX Queens
Before **nine** Bi-Polar Bears and
Sue Saw Caesar at the **zero** animal Zoo

* To aid memorizing a long string of numbers, consider creating a list of words that you don't numeralize. This allows you to construct sentences or poems instead of single words. Words like "*is, and, of, are, am, we, you, us, this, that, those, these,* and *the*" come to mind as particularly useful.
* When creating word associations it can sometimes be difficult to come up with words. Go through the list of

vowels one at a time, adding them to your letter until you find an appropriate word.
* Double-check your associations. It is easy to make a mistake and assign a number based on the presence of a letter instead of the phonetic value. It is also easy to confuse what letters are assigned to what numbers. In particular, I find I have a habit of assigning zero to the letter "O"… as opposed to the sibilant "S" and "C."
* Don't be all proper and shit when converting numbers to words. Use humor, puns, slang, or an association that has the most sensory links for you.

### Exercises

* Memorize the Number Association Chart.
* Come up with 10 words for the number 54. Use all vowel combinations for the first phonetic value. Fa, Fe, Fi, Fo, Fu.
* Create the numerical equivalents for the following words: Call, desk, cave, united, gem, cap, wail, diamond, knock, America, butcher, wire.
* Create words for the following numbers: 96, 58, 62, 86, 32, 21, 95, 187, 964, 832, 862, 846, 972, 794, 202, 104, 304, 307, 037, 215, 372, 654, 760.
* Select a short sentence and come up with the numeric value for all of its words.
* Use this system to memorize your phone number, a friend's phone number, and your checking account number.

### Memorize a Large Amount of Text

Two words: cipher it. By this I mean take your text and convert it to a simple cipher by using only the first and last letter of each word separated by a hyphen. On multi-syllabic words, you can use three letters. For simple words such as *"to, for,* and *the,"* use the whole word. If you were to cipher the first two sentences of the preceding paragraph it might look like this:

T-o w-s: c-r it. By this I m-n t-e y-r t-t and c-rt it to a s-e c-r by u-g o-y the f-t and l-t l-r of e-h w-d s-ed by a h-n.

When you use the cipher, you force your brain to *remember* each word in sequence instead of *read* each word. Enciphering the material does take a bit of time, but can cut your memorization time significantly. It is effective because you are automatically using memory muscles in addition to your reading muscles instead of reading text while trying to remember to memorize the information.

## Trigger Happy

Triggers are certain combinations of words, hand positions, and breathing patterns to which I've trained mind and body to respond. By associating these triggers with different physical, mental, or emotional states, I make it easier to achieve those states at will. Different magicians find different triggers to be useful. The trick is remembering to use the damn things in a stressful situation!

A trigger can combine Boot Camp elements of Visualization, Breathing, Self-Control, and Affirmations. We use the first two to create a link between the trigger and the desired response. Self-Control comes into play when we fire the trigger. Affirmations can be used prior to a trigger event to help us drill into our heads that we need to remember to fire it under stress. A few personal examples might help you get started.

When I was a young network administrator I had a job that consistently called me at 2 or 3 a.m. with problems that needed to be solved. I wasn't used to this, so I was very cranky about it. After a period of about 3 months, I trained myself to be more or less nice to the other person on the other end of the line until I could wake up enough to think clearly. Many years later, I created a mnemonic trigger that associated a finger gesture (No. Not THAT finger gesture) with the ring tone of the cell phone I used at the time. The finger trigger invokes my memory of the ring tone, which in turn prompts me to mentally respond, "I'm not clear headed and inclined to be nasty, but I'm going to be civil instead." I now try to use it when I'm caught completely off guard and inclined to be less than hospitable.

Remember the dish soap commercials that made the grease go to the edges of the sink when the soap was splooshed into the bowl? For some reason, it makes quite a useful focus for a mnemonic trigger. I associated a very classic occult gesture with this advertisement and visualize white light pushing negativity away from me when I use the hand gesture.

After partying hard one night, my friends and I started laughing very, very, very hard. For whatever reason, I remember a popping sensation in my head and thinking (in my not so sober state) that this must be what heaven was like. I use another set of gestures to remind myself of how I felt. I use this trigger to disrupt rather bad mental/emotional states. And yes, I also use it to apply Carroll's (1987) banishment by laughter.

Last, I also have a short list of mnemonics that use words, gestures, or body postures as the trigger. These are linked to the light trances, breathing patterns, and other altered states I achieve when I'm practicing my exercises. To create the link, I repeat the mnemonic words, make the gestures, or hold the body postures *while* I'm in the process of achieving those states or while I'm in those states. I use these triggers to quickly achieve a particular state. Sometimes I use them as short cuts to a trance during spell work, and sometimes I use them to disrupt the state in which I currently find myself.

You can use the preceding examples as a starting point to devise your own triggers. As you go about implementing them, pick words, phrases, gestures, or body postures you don't normally use, or only use during your Tower time. With spoken triggers, I tend to favor words and phrases spoken backwards. For example, "I am calm" becomes "M'lac ma I." After you have associated your trigger with the intended reaction, spend some time in meditation seeing yourself in stressful situations and remembering to invoke your trigger. You could also start repeating an affirmation to yourself that helps to reinforce the action you intend to take. Example Affirmation: Repeat "I remember to use my damned trigger when the situation warrants." Another affirmation might be as easy as, in the case of my first example, making the hand gesture, remembering the ring tone, and visualizing yourself being civil (and clearing your head as quickly as possible).

My most flexible triggers happen to be my magical alphabet, the Norse runes. By using them as an occult shorthand, I can highlight or suppress different facets of my life and the Reality around me. Different runes have different meanings that I have associated with different mental states or concepts. I invoke them by speaking the rune out loud or in my head. Usually I "speak" them in a magical way by exaggerating each syllable of the rune name in a tone of voice or pitch that I don't normally use. (Some folks call this vibrating). I get different shades of meaning by mixing and matching the runes as I deem appropriate. I am successful with this because I spent time in the Tower building my runic associations and binding them to triggers. (This means I had way too much free time, and it allowed me to meditate upon and memorize a whole bunch of Norse runes.)

## Tower Time

Time in my Tower is spent practicing traditional magic like casting spells or doing enchantments. Doing this classic form of magic in the Tower helps keep it from being immediate. This is a good thing, because I know I'm not completely in tune with the world or myself. Practicing magic means that I tacitly assume my Will manifests. Therefore, getting instant gratification might be worse for me than achieving something in a mundane fashion or getting nothing at all. Delaying magic this way creates a buffer zone for my Will and I give myself the opportunity to reflect on my Will and how it can best manifest.

To get the most out of our Tower time, we can divide it into three main phases of practice: Meditation, Self-Analysis and Spell Casting. Meditation can be as simple as breathing rhythmically or as difficult as stilling the mind or trying a demanding form of Eastern meditation. It teaches us how to change our mental and emotional state. Self-Analysis is fairly self-explanatory. It's the time taken to inventory where we've been, where we're at and where we are going... not to mention the Whys that lurk behind the scenes. Spell Casting is also pretty obvious. It's how we train ourselves to manifest Will in a safe, clear cut environment before venturing out to manifest that Will in a daily life that isn't quite so controlled.

## Conscientious Living and Paying Attention

When I was growing up, my dad always told me "Use your brain for something other than keeping your ears from falling into your chest cavity!" Though I'm quite sure he didn't mean for his maxim to be applied magically, I found ways to do just that. A good magician pays attention. A good magician finds ways to expand the scope of their attention. More data means a better understanding of the world. Because our Will manifests at all times we must pay attention to how we WANT it to manifest and how it is manifesting.

Because they are meant to manifest Will indirectly, the traditional use of ritual and spell tends to obfuscate the process of manifestation. The traditional forms were meant to help us pay attention to Will, then distill and purify it, and finally do what it takes to manifest it in accordance with our wishes. To many, ritual and spell somehow imply that we only have to talk the talk and not walk the walk. This is not the case! We first state our intentions via a spell, and then we follow up with action.

To make the distillation and manifestation of Will possible, many traditions train their students to engage in "conscientious living." They usually give fancy mystical reasons for engaging in this process, but there are purely pragmatic applications, too. A first step towards conscientious living, at least in the Western traditions, is to perform a set of daily adorations. For example: Golden Dawn tradition asks that the student perform scheduled adorations to the sun at sunrise, noon, sunset and midnight. It isn't as obvious, but many neo-pagan traditions do something similar with the eight seasonal Festivals and the full and new moon. Some (Rosicrucian and Druidic schools come to mind) have you review everything that happened during the day. Others have us wash our hands in a certain way and at certain times (Bardon). These varied activities have two things in common: they refocus our awareness towards the magical and give us the opportunity to step back just a moment and assess how well we are focused on being magical.

Viewed in this practical light, adorations make more sense. There isn't any inherent religiosity to it, it's a technique that takes our basic skills of meditation and stilling the mind and teaches us to do it in the real world. It's an intermediate step on the way to doing it in a situation that requires immediate action. And once we learn to step back slightly in practice, we're just a hop (skip and jump) away from acting instead of reacting.

Our scheduled mental pause does not have to be elaborate. Just a little time and effort can show that we mean magical business and that we're actively choosing to pay attention. After all, if I'm not paying attention then I'm not living magically. Practicing this mental pause provides a very important collateral skill–the ability to pause in stressful situations. By practicing the act of stepping back from our day in a non-stressful situation we prepare ourselves to do it in a stressful situation. *Acting* instead of *reacting* can make or break the Will cultivated in our Tower. Though, when I can get off my ass, I do find that a full-blown adoration helps because it means it's my choice to make my day magical... not the day's choice to make me magical.

A simple affirmation might be useful. Repeating the mantra "I pay attention" over and over again will pay off as the phrase sinks into our unconscious mind and we begin to do just that. Alternately a bare bones four times daily adoration can help too. In the morning when you wake up say something like "I salute the rising sun and the new day dawning. May it bring to healthy fruition the seeds planted the night before." At noon you might say, "I salute the zenith sun. May its light shine upon my endeavors and light the way so that I may see my obstacles and avoid them." In the evening a phrase like "As the sun sets, darkness descends. May I hold sunlight in my heart as wisdom reflecting the light of the moon," might be appropriate. Before going to bed "I put myself and my day to rest leaving that which was untoward in the dark and carrying forward the fruits of my labor that they might seed another dawning day."

## Personality Modification

Personality modification is the act of accenting parts of our personality when in different situations or with different people. It combines elements of Triggers, a complex exercise, with Self Control, a basic exercise. We do it every day in any case, so taking an active role in the process improves our magical lifestyle. Some magicians, like Carroll (1992), seem to suggest that we need completely separate personalities. My stance is that a similar effect can be obtained by identifying which traits we wish to put forward in certain situations. Then we find ways to trick, goad, or bribe ourselves into doing the ones that don't come naturally but fit what we've determined to be the best personality characteristics to apply in a given situation.

Triggers and Affirmations help quite a bit with this and take two forms. The first is a trigger intended to do nothing more than disrupt our current frame of mind. It might be a chant we use in our meditations or forcing ourselves to breathe calmly when it's the last reaction we really want to have. The second is a trigger associated with certain personality traits. Usually these are created by techniques like wearing certain clothes, holding our bodies a certain way, or wearing a ring we move to different fingers when we want to highlight certain attitudes, personality traits or reactions. Affirmations can be used to reinforce what we'd like ourselves to be so that when the time comes we do exactly what we intended to do.

## Personality Accents

Foreigners and their accents have always intrigued me. I've wondered how well they hear their accent in my tongue and how well I hear mine in theirs, and how non-native speakers cope with sounds that have no equivalent in their mother tongue. While listening to foreign speakers, I realized that personalities have accents, too: how we react to situations, the words we choose, our expressions of anger or frustration or delight or boredom. If we were never taught to hear something and don't react to it, that is a part of our personality accent, too. So, I decided to see if I could hear my personality language and then figure out which inflections and such were missing from my social "speech."

Once I began to listen to myself, much to my frustration, I heard the accents of those who most influenced my childhood or the accents of those that had done the most damage in my life. I heard how those accents interfered with what I was trying to accomplish. Once I started to hear them, it was time to modify my accent into something that was (at the very least) an action instead of a reaction by using "Jump Back Jack" techniques. This exercise is very difficult and I think its effectiveness will vary between practitioners.

To get started, use your Self-Control exercises to listen to yourself. Then use Perspective to view yourself as if you were someone else. Finally, use Self-Control to analyze the parts of yourself that you hear and to bring what you say and how you sound as a person more in line with what you'd like to hear.

## Jump Back Jack

Learning to Jump Back is the keystone of our Boot Camp Basics and the exercises in this chapter. It's the ability to act instead of react and it is a helluva lot easier in theory. Knowing that we are *reacting* instead of *acting* is only the first step. We have to be able to overcome our conditioned responses. Even when I knew I was reacting it just wasn't enough to get me to act the way I intended. I was stuck until I realized that the magical exercises I'd been drilling into my head for years could be used to accomplish this. Not thinking, focusing on a single thought, and breathing took on new meanings for me.

The first step is learning to identify the "monolithic thought state." Usually these are created by situations like being stressed out about bills or worrying about what I intended to say in a near future situation. In this state I tended to think about one thing to the exclusion of all else. This state can also be a narrowing of perceptions when the good old fight/flight response kicks in, or it can be the state we are in when we meet that new special someone in our life, or when we have something unexpected happen (good or bad). It's also the state of mind we get into when we are doing something creative or when we are meditating. "In the zone" or "flow" are phrases that come to mind.

Yes, I'm stating that even being in a state that is comfortable or feels good does not exempt us from stepping back to review it and ensure that it is where we need to be at that particular time. This is why I take lots of coffee breaks at work and, as a result, bathroom breaks. It's a religious thing. Really. Don't be messin' with my whole coffee/pee religion thing!

The second step is to learn to pull back from this state before it crowds out the ability to act. This takes a lot of work, and usually a fair amount of failure, before the jumping back takes hold. Those situations are particularly difficult because they are usually very stressful and a fight or flight response has taken over. Once fight or flight is on the table it's awfully damned difficult to tear myself away from those pre-programmed responses of self-preservation.

The final stage of Jump Back Jack is to remain in a state of awareness and give myself a chance to choose to act in any situation. I'm not there yet. I sometimes have it, and quite often lose it. In practice, I find I first react poorly to a situation, and then train myself to act differently to that situation, or similar situations, in the future. I never, ever seem to get it right the first time. Yet, as I reinforce my exercises and drill them further into my body and mind, I find that I'm holding on to this awareness and acting the way I want to in sticky situations. It's not a constant victory over my immediate reactions, but it is better than a poke in the eye with a sharp stick.

It's important to remember that these monolithic states are not necessarily bad. In fact, I'm not sure they can be eliminated. Fight or flight responses have served humans well a long time. So has creativity and single-mindedness. Of course, those things have also served us badly, too. The trick is to use this state consciously. This is difficult to do in high-pressure situations, but when we are alone with ourselves we have many tools at our disposal to practice getting a handle on our reactions. A good Jump Back Jack strategy teaches new habits for stressful situations and allows us to see them coming and act accordingly.

If I were to try and break out which Boot Camp exercises come into play with Jump Back Jack, I'd have to say all of them do, in one form or another. We can probably highlight Breathing to force a disruption in an unwanted emotional or physical state, Stilling the Mind to disrupt a mental state, and Affirmations as a "pre-incident" preparation to give us a tool to act instead of react. Triggers are quite useful here if we can create a few that are good at getting us to switch gears immediately.

## Paradigm Friction

I find that some level of constant friction between my personal belief system and the inflow of new ideas helps me to maintain a flexible state of mind. I suppose there are lots of ways to do it, but writing and reading are my primary tools because I read and write enough that I'm in a state of shifted awareness fairly often. Movies and television can also generate the requisite friction, though they can also put us in a passive trance state with no higher purpose than providing entertainment. That's not a bad thing; I just wanted to point out the risk. In any case, these activities can be used to define and build that liminal magical state without actually doing something I usually consider to be magical. Wikipedia ("Liminality," 2008 para. 2) defines liminality as *"characterized by ambiguity, openness, and indeterminacy. One's sense of identity dissolves to some extent, bringing about disorientation. Liminality is a period of transition where normal limits to thought, self-understanding, and behavior are relaxed – a situation which can lead to new perspectives."*

Achieving this state without a specific magical purpose is important because we keep the brain working on new ideas and new views of Reality. It's challenging and forces us to grow because we aren't seeking to reinforce our belief patterns. If we focus solely on solidifying what we already know, to the exclusion of self-development, we have ceased to be effective magically.

Reinforcement isn't a bad thing. It's needed to provide some sense of structure, but it can't be the only thing.

If we think of the liminal state as a lake with an inlet of fresh water and an outlet that releases excess volume, we begin to see how best to make this work. We want some form of change, but not so much that it damages the ecosystem. The damage might include disorientation or a counterproductive dissolution of self-identity. No change also damages the ecosystem. Think swamp.

Continual study of a single subject, excluding any new or external material, may lead to intellectual inbreeding. When this happens we establish a comfort zone that excludes personal growth and tend to reject data that doesn't reinforce our version of Reality. This severely limits our effectiveness because it creates a feedback loop that drowns out the new information we need to grow. The lack of fresh material can cause mutations in the mind that do not represent what the facts were intended to convey. These mutations masquerade as fact or as new ideas when, in reality, they only serve to bolster what we already know.

In contrast, studying subjects superficially, with no attempt to apply what we learn, indicates a lack of focus. Our liminal lake, or ecosystem, must balance quantity of material with practical application of the material. Too much information, without an appropriate outlet, and the lake floods. This is particularly true of magic. Practice must be a part of the equation for us to be effective, because reading about change isn't the same as changing. This doesn't mean we should avoid learning the basics about many different subjects. It means that after we've learned the theory, we ought to go that extra step and learn put that knowledge into practice when possible. Fictional wizards tend to have a vast array of knowledge balanced by a surprising amount of real world skills. There is more than a grain of truth in this knowledge/skill balance.

There is a lot of distraction in our daily lives. Most of it we put there ourselves. To cut out some of that distraction and achieve some semblance of liminality, I turn off the radio when driving. This eliminates a lot of numbing white noise and forces my mind to spend some time thinking. The act of driving provides just enough real world focus to keep my mind switching back and forth between being a vehicular menace to society and pondering different subjects.

At least once a week, I simply sit on my couch, usually with a notepad and pen handy, and think for an hour or so. Finally, when I take the occasional afternoon nap, I don't focus on falling asleep. I focus on reviewing my day while slipping into a very light sleep. More often than not I wake up an hour or so later with distinct memories of watching my mind REM sleep its way through sorting my experiences of the day. I rarely have a definite idea of what I "thought about" during my nap, but I inevitably wake up feeling a bit more grounded and mentally organized.

## Myth Friction

Mythology is a useful tool that helps me divine the underlying truth the stories try to embody and convey. One could also argue it also helps me make up my own truths about what a particular myth is trying to reveal. Many myths deal with the human condition. More importantly, I believe some mythological cycles attempt to deal with the limitations of humanity's subjective existence in the face of an unyielding and unsympathetic Reality. They personify portions of Reality that are not inherently human, a technique we use in the exercises on Self-Control.

Sometimes it helps me to think of a myth as one very large, complex symbol that has many meanings and associations. As I work with the different facets of this symbol, I find new ideas and meanings for each part. When I approach myth in this fashion, I find myself in a liminal state where, as I read and study the subject matter, I hear a second conversation in my head. It's a non-verbal subtext that conveys ideas to my conscious mind via the more visceral pathways of ideas. This allows me to work symbolically with these mythological concepts. It only seems to work well when I approach it with the intent of expanding my views rather than reinforcing them. I choose exploration rather than confirmation. To paraphrase Waite's translation of Levi (1974): Faith without some semblance of critical thinking is mere superstition.

As I reviewed my notes for some examples to present, I realized that my internal mythological structure was a syncretic amalgam of original source material and my own ideas. It was difficult to pull out undiluted strains of myth from my head and provide isolated examples you could build upon. So, I'm going to present you with an example of the end result of my studies and hope this gives you an idea or two for your own experiments in this area.

## Collen's M3SNA
### (Modern Syncretic Morass of Norse Mythology and its Application)

At the root of my mythological investigations is my "World Tree." I use Yggdrassil, the Norse Tree of Life, to help me categorize and understand various metaphorical truths. It is a geometric structure that symbolically represents my internal and external cosmos. I use various meditative, Astral and scrying techniques when working with Yggdrassil.

Yggrdassil as a construct contains two primary building blocks, Worlds and Pathways. In my system, the Worlds are nine realms connected by 11 Pathways, though most modern occultists use 24. I'm either lazy or inclined to Base 10 representations of binary numbers, take your pick. Each World is a facet of the World Tree, and can be conceptualized as very much like different countries on Earth.

Each world has inhabitants, culture, and history. Like one of the four classic Elements, a World holds a large set of associations, meanings, and symbolism that I interact with and expand upon. Each World, like each Element, is associated with different god forms, runes, and symbolism. I work with these Worlds by traveling to them and exploring them during my meditations.

A Pathway is a connection, or bridge, between two Worlds. Generally, a Pathway holds symbolism related to the two Worlds it connects and any concepts deriving from that connection. Pathways symbolize a magician's movement between different perspectives and the ability to come to grips with his/her Reality by experiencing it from different points of view. As I travel these Pathways, I transition to different world-views. I reflect upon how the different ideas contained within each World can interact with or oppose each other. In other words, moving between Worlds means I am in the process of changing perspective.

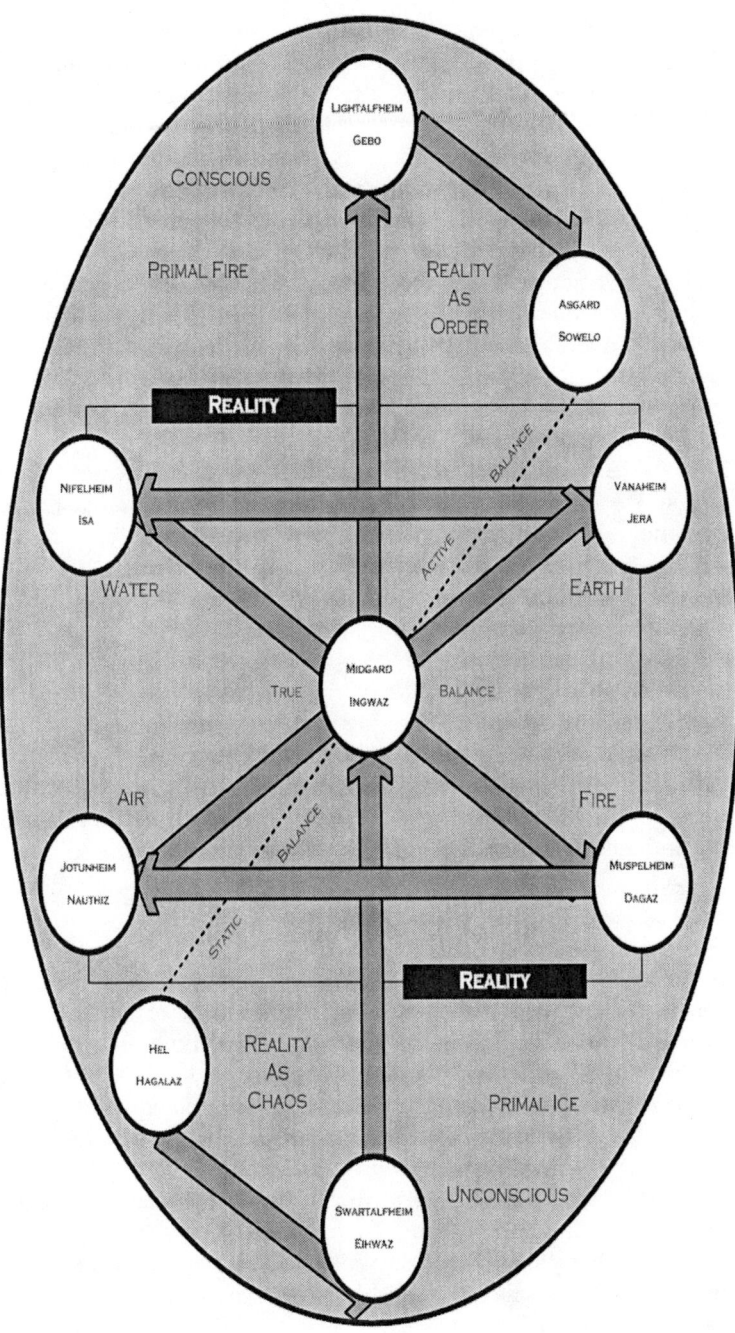

In my World Tree, I use the Eihwaz and Dagaz runes as the "shape" for my tree. They describe the Pathways and the relationship the Worlds have with each other. Eihwaz is a rune commonly associated with Yggdrassil. Dagaz, with its meanings of day, cycle, division, and balance, holds appropriate symbolism for Midgard and its associated Worlds. Note that, due to the two-dimensional nature of the diagram, it is impossible to convey the three-dimensional structure of the tree; Asgard and Hel are very close to each other (as if they curved around the backside of the oval) and not at opposite ends of the tree. Ratatosk the squirrel tends to symbolically support this arrangement when he brings tidbits of news from the eagle on top to the serpent Niddhog beneath (Bellows, 1936).

Eihwaz

At its most basic, my World Tree maps a journey which starts in the unformed Chaos of Hel, moves into the first stages of form and substance in Swartalfheim, manifests in Self or Midgard, then begins a journey of manifestation through the middle worlds of Reality. Once the transit of Reality is complete, this stage of the journey can end in Midgard or move into the realm of enlightenment, or Lightalfheim. From there it transcends into Asgard. In Asgard, the journey doesn't end; instead, it finds itself in Hel ready to begin the next higher level of transformation. This concept of the highest level of the tree being the lowest level of another higher tree, and vice versa, can be found in Qabalistic teachings.

Dagaz

## Circuit Magic

Circuit magic encompasses some techniques I've developed to control magical manifestation using the concept of an electrical circuit. The thinking that went into these methods went something like this: Sooner or later, I'm going to be really good at manifesting Will. If I'm not careful, I might find I've manifested something that wasn't what was best for me. Alternately, I might not manifest Will properly when I wasn't aware I needed it.

I do a lot of spell casting in my head and have created an imaginary ritual chamber for that purpose. In said chamber is a holder I've created for my staff, which sits in a special case and is connected via a socket to magical power. To keep my Will from manifesting when I don't want it to, I remove the staff from its case. When the staff is out magic cannot manifest, unless I consciously pick up the staff and use it myself. For magic to manifest automatically, I put the staff back.

How you implement the ability to control your magic may vary. In the end, you want to set a trigger that allows you to mentally activate or de-activate magic at Will. This can be done mentally, as I do, or in the material world, such as by placing some Implement of Significance in a particular place and moving it somewhere else when circumstances dictate.

### Short Circuit

> I have a little birdy on my shoulder.
> *Tweet.*
> He doesn't seem to get much older.
> *Tweet.*
> But he does whisper in my ear words of cupidity
> that keep me from committing unwanted acts of stupidity.
> *Tweedle-dee-deet.*

In other words, I created a visualization that is designed to short circuit any magical manifestation from happening when I don't want it to happen. I build upon the imagery of the previous circuit by placing a fuse between the case that holds my staff and the magical energy. This fuse is hooked up to my emotional and mental states. If my emotional or mental energies get out of hand, the fuse blows and I have to replace it before I can push more Will through the circuit. It keeps me from getting out of control magically when I'm overly excited, happy, sad, tired, or angry.

### Smart Circuit

There are two types of Smart Circuit. Both deal with incorporeal allies, such as spirits or deities. The first circuit is controlled by someone more knowledgeable than I am. To wit, my spirit guide and patron deity are empowered to manifest magic for me when needed and when I'm not smart enough to know it's needed. They also short-circuit my magic when it's the wrong answer to the problem. In short, when it is in my best interest, they are allowed to yank my staff out of its case or blow my fuse when they feel it is in my best interests. They can also hook the staff back up when I've pulled it out and magic really needs to be manifesting at that particular moment. (There's something about the goddess Isis and the phrase "blow my fuse" I find sophomorically amusing. But then I think about Osiris's unattached, wrinkled dinky and it isn't quite so funny any more.)

The second looks suspiciously like praying to one's deity. By saying the magical equivalent of "Thy Will be Done" I acknowledge my fallibility and give my Will a way out of manifesting exactly as specified. Especially when, in the deep dark recesses of my mind, I know that the outcome is either bad for me or that there is a better way for my Will to manifest. This does require a relationship with deity or the creation of an egregore for the purpose, though I'm sure an atheist magician could come up with a way to implement this that isn't predicated on a godform. Oh, and I actually do say, "Thy Will be Done." You might find a different phrase to be more appropriate.

# Chapter Three: It's Just a Theory

Most traditions assume that magical skill is a factor in the magical process. If this is always true, then our first spells ought to do nothing at all. It intrigues me that beginners often have success in their initial attempts at magic and that spells consistently work in the face of minimal training. To reconcile these discrepancies, I decided that magic *always* works because Will *always* manifests. Will, being willful, does not always do what we want it to, but it always does something. Looked at from that perspective, magic is a way to distill and direct Will as opposed to actually creating some new sort of Will. In fact, if a Will already exists it cannot be created. I suppose it can be recreated, but then it isn't the same Will.

As I present my ideas on Will and magic, keep in mind that I think of them as an interface, or skin, used to work with magic. They aren't a single one size fits all paradigm. It's a way to put some sort of structure on a concept that seems to defy and welcome structure at the same time.

## Principle of Will

*"Will manifests."*

It's that simple. Will *always* manifests. This is why it is so important to understand Self. The more I know the better I am at manifesting Will in an expected manner. By extension, it is important to understand how a Will not my own manifests because those Wills can still help or hinder my Will. This might help explain why, no matter how well trained we are, Will sometimes does not manifest the way we intended.

Will is closely tied to the concept of momentum. In science, momentum is an object's mass multiplied by its velocity. In my magical terms, it is potential that has been put in motion, and can apply to feelings, thoughts, and actions. It applies to physical objects like rocks rolling down hills and also applies to visceral concepts, like the power the laws of my country have over me. These things are Will in action and, to different degrees, they affect me and I affect them.

Will and Momentum are sometimes indistinguishable from each other. To help clarify this, let's look at two definitions. The first is from *The Kybalion* (The Three Initiates, 1912. p. 10). In it there is a principle, known as the Principle of Vibration, which states, *"Nothing rests; everything moves; everything vibrates."* Our second is a paraphrase of Newton's Laws of Motion from Wikipedia (2008). Newton's Laws of Motion): *"Objects in motion, or at rest, tend to stay that way unless some external force acts on them; Objects move in straight lines unless something diverts them; and all actions have equal and opposite reactions."* If I take the first two thirds of the Kybalion's definition, *"Nothing rests, everything moves"* and meld it with my layman's summary of Newton's Laws *"A Will in motion tends to remain in motion unless an external force acts upon it"* we better understand why Will and Momentum are thick as thieves. Momentum isn't Will, but because Will is perpetually in motion it always has Momentum.

This leads us into the Principle of Momentum. Momentum can be an external outside influence that changes my results, or *my* influence changing the course of external events. Basically, if I know who I am, know what I want, understand what it takes to get there and act accordingly, then the chances are good that I will get exactly what I expected.

## Principle of Momentum

*"Momentum counts."*

To rephrase the Newtonian terms from above, a Will in motion tends to stay in motion and a Will at rest tends to stay at rest. Action and inaction are different states of Will. Depending on the situation, action, inaction, rest, and movement may be neutral, good, or bad for the magician. The effects of a certain state of Momentum depend on the circumstances in which those effects are present. In other words, like states increase the probability of like events. This is basically a restatement of the Hermetic Principle of "As above, so below." By surrounding myself with certain people, places, and things, I build Momentum in certain directions. Thinking and feeling certain things builds momentum. Performing certain actions builds momentum.

The principle of Momentum applies across all spectrums of existence. Momentum can potentially be modified or changed but it cannot be bypassed or ignored. Example: Someone fires a pistol at me. The bullet speeding towards my head trumps any hasty last minute spell (or gibbered prayer) for my safety. The physical momentum of the bullet outweighs any mental force I apply to changing its direction. In this example, a proper application of Will and Momentum is to be in touch with my surroundings and myself so that I never wind up in such a dangerous situation. Using my Will and Momentum to generate and maintain a situation of safety is much more desirable than trying to reshape events that have moved out of my control. And yes, as magicians we can save ourselves a lot of grief by admitting that some things are out of our control, or have moved out of our control, cut our losses and get the hell out of Dodge.

## Principle of Defaults

*"Know yourself, know your result."*

I'm a computer guy so I work with terms that make sense to me. This principle derives from the term "Default Settings," which comes from the computer world and is what a piece of software or hardware does if I don't tell it to do something different. This concept applies in magic, too. It's what I am capable of without any extra effort. Of course, changing myself isn't as simple as clicking a check box, but it is up to me, the magician, to find those internal check boxes by hook or by crook and change them accordingly.

The Principle of Defaults is concerned with knowing who and what I am as well as what I am capable of. This Principle takes into consideration my Momentum, the ongoing manifestation of my Will, what I *do know* about my current "state," and what I *do not know* or understand. This Principle is used to define the manner in which my Will manifests when I have not explicitly specified how it should manifest. In other words, this principle describes what will most likely happen when I am guilty of the following:

* Not paying attention.
* Misunderstanding or not knowing my Default Settings.
* Misunderstanding the Principle of Momentum.
* Not understanding the implications of manifesting Will.
* Reacting instead of acting.

Applying this principle encourages awareness and expands our ability to work with the Data Stream. We want to work from a vantage point of informed decision as often as possible. Unfortunately, the infinite complexity of the universe is subject to infinite interpretation and there is no limit to what we don't know. This realization was discouraging to me at first, but when I finally accepted that I didn't know everything, nor fully understand the things I did know, I took a big step forward in my magical thinking.

## Principle of Reality

*"There is an objective Reality.*
*We can only experience it with our mind.*
*The human mind is subjective."*
Full Stop.

Those four lines have deep implications if we decide to take them seriously. Accepting the idea that there is an Objective Reality, which we can only experience subjectively, is a big responsibility. It means we've accepted a worldview that we can't possibly master, because objectivity and subjectivity are at constant odds with each other. It's our job to do the best we can with a difficult situation.

There is infinite data and infinite experience. There is no one definition that conclusively pins down magic, life, person, experience, or piece of information. No one viewpoint encompasses everything that we see or experience, and we can always improve on the amount of information we pluck from the Data Stream. We can imagine our perspective as a box. What we comprehend falls within the confines of that box and is linked to an infinite amount of information outside of the box.

Acceptance of this principle is an admission of defeat. We acknowledge and accept that we can't know everything. However, this defeat creates opportunities for immense success. Knowing our limits, working on them, and integrating them into our being can give us an edge most people do not have. Knowing our limits means we know who we are. Integrating those limits makes us comfortable with who we are. These two facts alone can give us the ability to live life to its fullest without being so desperately attached to life that we are owned by life itself.

Because the human mind is subjective and Reality is objective, tension arises between the internal world of the magician and the external world with which the magician works. In traditional spell casting, the magician willfully creates this tension by highlighting this conflict (what is vs. what we want) during the magical process. When the tension is released, the potential energy becomes Momentum and the spell is activated. However, magic can be extended beyond the tension/release cycle to become a way to work with the disparity of what *is* versus what we *perceive*. In this context, magic is a tool we use to come to grips with how we interact with our world. Because we are subjective creatures, this magical interaction depends on how we define Reality.

To understand this tension and find ways to work with it, we can break our personal Reality into three parts: Verbal Reality, Non-Verbal Reality, and Reality proper. Reality exists independent of our minds; it exists even if we don't exist. The Universe operates according to rules, even if we don't know or understand them.

There is also a Reality that exists inside of our minds. This Reality also has rules. However, our Internal Reality is subjective, flexible, and encompasses both verbal and non-verbal Reality. How we come to understand them, work with, and reconcile these disparities defines who we are as people and as magicians.

## Verbal Reality or Verbal Filter

The first type of Reality is not actually a Reality; it is a filter. It has a lot in common with the psychic censor of Chaos Magic. Verbal Reality uses words to represent Reality, and words are filters. Unfortunately, we tend to assume that this language filter *is* Reality. In point of fact, our Verbal Filter has developed to the point that it can be considered a Reality in its own right. It is subjective, though it perversely manages to masquerade as objective Reality more often than not. In this section I may refer to Verbal Reality as the Verbal Mind, Verbal Filter, a Verbal Overlay, or Verbal Consciousness. Each term highlights different facets of the same concept.

The strength of the verbal filter is that, by assigning portable words to large concepts, it makes working with ideas manageable. For example, the word house does not convey the true meaning of what a house is. The Reality behind what a house represents is more complex. However, it is much easier to converse using this "reality shorthand" than it is to attempt to cover everything a house is every time one's domicile is discussed. The weakness of this approach is that it tends to become, and thereby restrict, the amount of Reality with which we can work. If we insist that a dictionary's definition of house is a house and then ignore the macrocosmic Reality in favor of a portable microcosmic word, we are constrained by our verbal subjectivity.

## Non-Verbal Reality

The Non-Verbal Mind is our true Internal Reality and is comprised of much more than words and language. It is who we really are and contains both objective and subjective information: who we are and who we subjectively *think* we are. The Non-Verbal Mind corresponds to the psychological concepts of the subconscious mind. It is important to remember that we can be non-verbally aware of information, too. Unlike the Verbal Mind, The Non-Verbal Mind is non-linear and macrocosmic.

Because our internal Reality is non-verbal and this contains who we really are, it has a link with Reality, which is also non-verbal. This link gives our Non-Verbal Mind direct access to the Data Stream. In a sense, the subconscious/Non-Verbal Mind is the information and the conscious/Verbal Mind is how we use it. By limiting the influx of data, Verbal Filters, as a function of what we call sanity, make it easier for us to work in the "real world."

## Working With Reality

Reality exists, is non-verbal, and doesn't give a hoot about how well we interact with it or how much information we train ourselves to cope with. Our Non-Verbal Mind has the ability to interact with Reality objectively via the Data Stream *and* subjectively via its interpretations of the Data Stream. The key to working with Reality is this objective/subjective bridge created by our Non-Verbal Reality. This bridge by no means comes to terms with what Reality is, but relates to Reality more accurately than our day-to-day verbal labels.

Our three Realities intertwine and influence each other. Verbal Consciousness is very effective (and very appropriate) for many situations and tasks, but can be a stumbling block to effective magic. Communicating with our conscious mind is easy. We use words. Speaking with our subconscious mind is more difficult because it is non-verbal and we are comfortable using speech to interact with our world and ourselves. To make things complicated, there is no clear line between these two states of awareness. At some point, these states cross and blend together. The process of dealing with this information and the data flow is difficult because:

a. the act of observing how we do this generally engages our conscious mind only and

b. each form, whether verbal or non-verbal, uses different methods and means to communicate.

Our Non-Verbal Reality can be spoken with, but to be effective this "speech" must be indirect (or Non-Verbal) to prevent our Verbal Filters from altering the information in such a way that interaction with our Non-Verbal Reality becomes meaningless. Conversely, this "speech" must also be capable of presenting meaningful information in manageable chunks from our Non-Verbal Reality to our Verbal Reality so that we can comprehend and work with the information. Tension arises between the Verbal and Non-Verbal because the Verbal Filter limits the data. Tension is released and momentum created when we bypass the verbal filter and access the Data Stream directly.

For example: translation using literal terms can destroy the original meaning. An analogy would be translating a book from French into English. A good translator does more than simply translate the text literally. They compensate for the difference in language and culture by matching up meanings and not just words. They rework allusions and know how to evoke the correct *effect* in the destination language. Something still gets lost, but the reader gets a fairly accurate representation of the original information.

Because of this disparity between *what is, what is perceived, and what is altered by the act of perceiving* we need a method of working with information that moves data from verbal to non-verbal states in such a way that the least amount of data is lost. This method is sometimes referred to as magic (in its myriad disciplines) and used to link together verbal and non-verbal information. Once that is accomplished, we then use that link to affect our internal Non-Verbal Reality. Once we do that, we can

### It's Just a Theory

affect Reality itself because we have established a direct link to it via our tie to the Data Stream.

Magic uses various disciplines to work with our inner and outer Reality. These techniques are artificial constructs designed to create our own internal language that bridges these different Realities. By using this constructed "language" we create a middle ground between our conscious (verbal) and subconscious (non-verbal) minds and get them both to agree on that middle ground. Every single one of us is different; therefore that middle ground varies wildly for each one of us. The exact same symbols or methods have different (if sometimes related) meanings for each individual.

Spellcasting is a powerful example of this. This is not because of the spell, but how it functions. It operates by modifying or bypassing our Verbal Reality and linking with Non-Verbal Reality. I'm not going to name any particular system that does this unabashedly, but its initials are Chaos Sigil Magic. (I assume you already know about Sigil Magic. If not, skip to People Sigil Magic in the chapter The Obligatory Grimoire for a quick overview.) Sigil Magic is powerful because Sigils become non-verbal signifiers that operate via Non-Verbal Reality. As such, they have direct access to the Data Stream. This highlights that fact that not all spells, Chaos or otherwise, have to be put to words to be put into effect in Reality. We've got a winner as long as the sucker reaches Non-Verbal Reality where it can be pumped straight into the Data Stream. A spell is a symbolic label (which might be words or something more abstract) that taps the Reality we are trying to create.

Some examples that might help give you insight into how this works:

> * Spells and Divination are different sides of the same coin. Spells take verbal representations of Will, translate it into non-verbal form, and inject the information into the Data Stream. Divination pulls non-verbal data from the stream and translates it into verbal information. The trick to both is to make the conversion without mangling the data to the point it becomes useless. Magic is flexible enough that the obverse of each can be true as well— we can use spell work to shift non-verbal data to verbal and Divination to translate verbal information to non-verbal.

* Though we use microcosmic verbal components, a spell embodies a lot of macrocosmic non-verbal wishes and desires. It is an attempt to manifest a wish symbolically and provides a level of flexibility and potential that merely stating what we want cannot do. Its power resides in the effects of opening ourselves to the potential of the macrocosm while not restricting our possibilities by focusing on portions of the microcosm. Trees, meet forest.
* Divination relates to the three Realities much like dreams relate to the waking world. Let's say that a car outside your window is honking its horn while you sleep. Your dream state incorporates that into your dream. It may manifest as a horn honking. It may be geese flying overhead. It may take the form of a person talking. While dreaming, whatever the representation is, you are physically hearing sounds. Subjectively, it may not register in your mind at all (in which case you sleep like the dead). Your dream state does NOT change the Reality that some fool is laying on the horn outside your window. Your dream state takes that fact and dresses it with information from your own library of Non-Verbal references.
* The previous example illustrates how fluid our interpretations of Reality can be. However, unlike being in a dream state, when we perform a divination we are fully aware of what takes place, though we may not fully understand the information that comes to light. Let's say you toss a Celtic Cross spread using the Tarot. Whether you say it out loud or just think it in your mind, you are *consciously* asking a question.

This is an attempt to tap into the non-verbal Data Stream and obtain information we can consciously put to good use. If we are successful, our Non-Verbal Mind answers with the facts of which it is aware. We then use the intermediate "language" of Tarot symbolism to present that information to our Verbal Mind. This "language" is the bridge between Non-Verbal and Verbal that allows them to communicate with one another.

Because information does tend to get lost in translation, whether due to our conscious desire to get a particular answer or because we have a "middle man" between verbal and non-verbal, our final interpretation doesn't necessarily change or accurately represent Reality... much like how we might perceive geese in a dream.

## Placebo Magic

The preceding Principles present a framework for applying magic, but they don't define what magic is. There doesn't seem to be a single definition of magic that is clear and concise, but I can safely say that approaching magic in a linear fashion expecting a linear result is flawed. It's about averages and not absolutes. Living magically works best when we look at the whole picture and not a single instance of cause and effect. To bring that picture into focus, I have a very short definition for magic: magic is leverage. Placebo Magic explains this leverage metaphorically by encompassing the lever, fulcrum, and object being acted upon, as well as how we utilize those things.

In Placebo Magic, Reality is the fulcrum. The lever is our subjectivity and the object we are trying to move is the situation we are trying to change. Our Will is the amount of force we apply to the lever. That force can be augmented or diminished by our Momentum. Of course, as in all things magical, everything is a bit more slippery than these streamlined ideas imply.

Magic appears to be the direct cause of a sequence of events when it is not. In truth, magic causes change in a manner that is symbolically removed from Reality, just as our perception and perspective is removed from Reality. Rather than be hamstrung by this seemingly insurmountable difficulty, we can use our subjectivity to overcome the obstacle. Magic in this application now has striking parallels to a placebo because we are willfully modifying our perceptions of the world to get results. This change

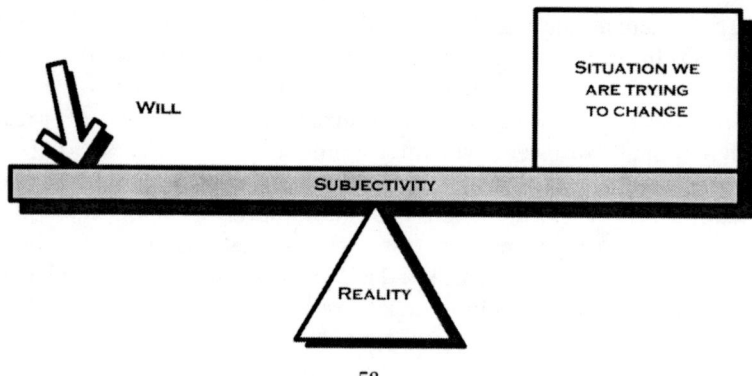

redirects our awareness into channels that are beneficial to us and creates new opportunities for our Will to manifest.

When we think of a placebo, we think of a sugar or starch pill given to a patient to treat a symptom, while telling the patient that the pill is "real medicine." The patient subsequently gets better. This is an effective use of a placebo, as it causes change that can be measured. When we give ourselves, or someone else for that matter, a catalyst for change (the metaphoric placebo) we have accomplished something. We've used Reality as a fulcrum and leveraged our subjectivity to foster an awareness of more options. This makes it more likely that we can successfully complete a desired course of action.

When we cast a placebo spell we are fully aware that we are bypassing our doubts. We do this to implant new possibilities and convince ourselves that the prospects for success are real. In placebo terms, we believe we are ill. The magic pill helps us to believe we can get better. Sometimes we do get better. This is not because of the pill and precisely because we choose to take the pill.

Having more opportunities also means we also have more ways to fail. This is why looking at magic as a system of *averages* instead of *absolutes* is important. The trick to this whole magic/placebo/lever paradigm is to transform the nebulous opportunities we've created, by leveraging subjectivity, into concrete goals and action.

It's worth noting that using Reality as the fulcrum has its drawbacks because, like it or not, "Will Manifests." If we attempt to manifest our Will without understanding the implications of who we are, magic might seize on non-verbal fears or restraints and manifest those instead. There is no rule that says the placebo we inject into our Data Stream is the one we think we injected. This is why we use every means possible to heighten our awareness, keep tabs on ourselves, and get to know ourselves. We must do this to get consistent and positive results from our work. Besides, it's damned uncomfortable when we insert the placebo in the wrong end of the Data Stream.

Most folks scoff at placebos. They say, "*It was false. It was in the mind. It didn't help the person to get better. They did it themselves. That patient was silly.*" And yet... the patient *did get better*. The patient *did* do it themselves. (However, the patient may still be just as silly.)

By extension, it is quite easy for a magician to scorn the placebo-like qualities of taking advantage of our subjectivity. This is because we have been conditioned by popular culture to expect a very literal and showy form of magic based on absolutes. It's disappointing to think of magic as an indirect player or a metaphor. Modern mindsets want concrete proof and validation. These can be had. However, magic rarely manifests directly in the mundane world because it generally cannot do so. It must manifest within us first. Magical proof and validation come afterwards and are enjoyed indirectly via the success of our actions. Faith without works is dead and we must first consider something to be possible before attempting it.

Striving to prove that magic works isn't the same as practicing magic. It is an indictment of our need to be validated. To be an effective magician we do not *need* that validation. We *want* results. If viewing magic as placebo gets results, so be it. We acknowledge it for the success it brings while know that it does so indirectly by manifesting through us.

Considering magic as a placebo keeps us safer than approaching magic literally. Magic becomes a figurative and philosophic process. By taking this point of view, we give ourselves the ability to stand back and ask ourselves "Is it working? Or is it a suppository?" When we ask ourselves this, we force ourselves to look at how well we are leveraging our awareness to affect Reality. Then we adjust accordingly... possibly even to the point of abandoning a particular course of action. In other words, rather than spending precious time and energy trying to force Reality to conform to the idea that magic is literal energy, we allow our magic to integrate with Reality via subjectivity.

What about cases where magic clearly and directly manifests in the real world? You've got me, there. It is a big universe with lots of possibilities. However, most good magicians work within the realm of *their* possibilities and really good magicians keep finding ways to expand those possibilities.

# Chapter 4: Ruh-Roh, Raggy

I've noticed that when my spells fail they have this uncanny knack of rubbing something personal about the failure in my face when they go wrong. At first, this seems like an outright attack by my supposed friend magic. Bad magic. No goat. Yet, as I thought about it I realized that magic was doing exactly what was expected of it. It highlighted my Will and made it manifest, just not in the way I wanted.

The irony was that the spell had not backfired. Rather, it looked that way to me because I was thinking in terms of magic being energy when I cast my spell. What magic really did was highlight Will using ideas like energy and power. Because my Will was illuminated in a way I had not anticipated, it seemed as though magic deliberately slapped me in the face. I wasn't prepared. I got boxed about my ears.

Life is complex. Because of that, or in spite of it, magic has a tendency to manifest through the shortest route. That short, easy route is often down the superhighway of our ingrained habits and traits. Momentum doesn't make an exception for what we don't like about ourselves, nor for the things we've put in motion while we weren't paying attention. Remember Momentum? We should take pains to make nice with our Momentum. It's pretty safe to say that magic works, it doesn't necessarily manifest in the manner we intended or expected, and that if magic really made it a habit of manifesting immediately we'd be in some serious doo doo. The risk in magical practice isn't that magic works. It's that Will can't be unplugged. It can't be stopped. The good part is that Will can be changed and consistently working with magic tends to bring our Will under some semblance of control.

We can't avoid the repercussions of exposing our Will when we practice magic. The whole magic as power thing might obfuscate what happened, but it doesn't *change* what happened. To help clear up the situation, I started a list of different things that can jump out and bite us when we shake our magical thang.

## Self

Because magic exposes our Will, difficulties sometimes ensue because, sooner or later, we stumble upon who we really are sneaking about in our Non-Verbal Reality and eating raw fish in the dark. If we think of magic in terms of literal energy, that stumble can turn into a nasty fall because the manipulation of energy isn't what magic is ultimately about. It's about self-knowledge. I'm not talking about knowing yourself in some warm fuzzy kind of way either. I'm talking about knowing that mean, nasty ol' creature lurking somewhere inside us that magic has this uncanny knack of finding. That being said, who we are isn't wrong. It just is. But what we do with ourselves and why we do it has consequences, for better or worse.

The dark truth of Self is not something we want to share with anyone. It's not comfortable, it's not glamorous, and it certainly isn't exciting. It's painful and embarrassing. It's horrifying. It makes us want to cringe over what we are or what we've done or what we've let happen. It makes me want to hide... forever. We want to scream in abject defeat because... *da dad dum*, it's the honest truth. Even worse, it isn't just *what we are* but *why we are that way*. Nobody likes to know that. Even fewer go looking for it. But when we practice magic, we tacitly acknowledge this quest.

The difficult part of this process is that even AFTER we find this garish core of Self, begin to come to terms with it, embrace the quest, and decide to change it for the better, it's a nickel-plated bitch to actually change. After all, it's at the innermost core of everything we do! Tearing out that core rips out the heart of the web that spins our self-identity. And not being who we are isn't the goal.

Luckily, practicing magic limbers us up mentally, emotionally, and spiritually for the demands this quest places upon us. Even better, most of us get the questionable privilege of working our ass off for a lot of years before suffering the consequences of our quest. Because it takes a while to find Self (or at least figure out we are looking for it), by the time we find it we are already magically trained to some degree. Of course, this also means that the longer we practice the more likely it is that we will trip over our fugly (fucking ugly, for the slang impaired) Self. But, by the time we fall down and pick ourselves back up, we realize that some of the changes have already occurred and we don't feel quite so icky about the situation.

Some make it through the quest. Others don't. None come away unscathed. But magic, being the flexible creature it is, does make the process bearable and worth doing. What is unfortunate is that few magical systems state the details of the process clearly. Cast a spell, be a better person. Astrally project, be a better person. Worship the Goddess, be a better person. These things are all worthwhile, but they don't get at acknowledging who we are. And if magic is about manifesting Will, any magician worth their salt had better damn well know where that Will comes from.

Will comes from the lifetime of experiences we've accumulated. Not all of those experiences were light and wonderful. They weren't necessarily bad, but can be bad for us now if we don't make our best attempt to look at them objectively. It isn't easy. Though I most certainly have not crossed Crowley's abyss, certain parts of myself have died and been reborn. In short, if I had not been forced to question everything about myself, I would not have changed a thing. I would not have been flexible enough to use magic effectively, and I would not have been able to honestly call myself a magician. It took over six years for me to get to a point where I felt like I had *started*. It is still going on. Your mileage may vary.

Ancient myth can be used as a roadmap on the Self Quest. The descent of the Sumerian goddess Inanna into the underworld is a symbolic story of this process commonly explored by magicians. Whether or not it was originally intended this way I'll leave to the scholars. Inanna decides she wants to visit the underworld to attend her brother-in-law's funeral. Her sister, Ereshkigal, rules the underworld. She gets elaborately dressed up for her visit. But at each of the seven gates she is required to remove an article of clothing or jewelry until she finds herself in front of her sister standing naked (I am from Kansas. This word is pronounced NEKKED. Move along. Move along.). What happens next is quite interesting.

> *After she had crouched down and had her clothes removed, they were carried away. Then she made her sister Erec-ki-gala rise from her throne, and instead she sat on her throne. The Anuna, the seven judges, rendered their decision against her. They looked at her -- it was the look of death. They spoke to her -- it was the speech of anger. They shouted at her -- it was the shout of heavy guilt. The afflicted woman was turned into a corpse. And the corpse was hung on a hook. (Black, J.A. &*

Cunningham, G. & Fluckiger-Hawker, E & Robson, E. & Zólyomi, G. 1998. Lines 164 to 172.).

From a very early age we learn to build layers of personality and ego shells around ourselves. Not all of these shells are good. To complicate matters, it isn't easy to strip those shells away or part them long enough to understand where they fit into who we are. The shouts of guilt, speech of anger, affliction and death all point to the difficulties inherent in this quest of self-knowledge.

We still need to get to the heart of Self. However, we need to do this as carefully as possible because aggressively ripping our layers away can leave our internal landscape in tatters. Like the liminal states in the previous chapter, we are an ecosystem with its own balance and needs. There is a big difference between firing up an emotional DC 9 Caterpillar tractor and walking into our eco-selves with a set of pruning shears. Approaching who we are with respect, care, a sense of responsibility and balance gives us the opportunity to work with these layers constructively. *Constructive* is the key word here. The intent should be to make ourselves better people by working with who we are, not tearing out who we are while thinking an internal bulldozing inherently makes for a better person. This process is about gentle integration, not dictatorial control or punishment.

If we step back and look at the exercises in this book, the intent is to respectfully get at the roots of who we are and, more importantly, why we are that way. It's worth mentioning that even if someone else is to blame, blaming another short circuits the process. At some point, we have to take responsibility, not so much for what was done to us but what we did and are still doing with the repercussions. For good or ill, we had a choice in our actions during the aftermath. (In case you were wondering, Enki saves her. Good ol' Enki.)

### Bleed Through

Magical Bleed Through is not a good thing. It is a normal result of magical practice, so it isn't a bad thing unless we ignore it. It's the mental and spiritual equivalent of fatigue. It can be looked at as a warning that we are spending too much time practicing magic and not enough time living it. It has many symptoms and they can include:

* Not being sure whether you dreamed it or really did it.
* Tower work consistently being disrupted by bad or disturbing "visions."
* The inability to focus, visualize, or concentrate when meditating or entering altered states of consciousness. This might also be a sign of ordinary fatigue or other normal factors.
* Having disturbing visions during normal waking that may or may not cause a physical reaction. (For example: Flinching, cringing, or tensing up.)
* Working solely in the Tower to the exclusion of all other endeavors is a sure sign of bleed through (obsession, actually... but the warning fits well here.)

The easiest way to fix it is to take a break. If a short break does not do the trick then try to clearly delineate between your Tower sessions and normal activity. This might take the form of avoiding magical work immediately prior to going to bed, or giving yourself at least a two-hour buffer between magical work and sleep. You can also construct the magical circuits from Boot Camp basics to give yourself some extra leeway. If you do a lot of magic in your head, try moving any spell work into the material world until the Bleed Through subsides. Do all magical work within the context of a full ritual so that you are clearly delineating between mundane and magical space.

When you do the full ritual, focus on the semantics of switching to and from the magical state. This includes giving extra importance to donning ritual garb, or meditating prior to the ritual, or possibly taking extra care to focus on the preliminary stages of your work. If you don't normally cast a circle or purge your space before beginning, doing these things reinforces the transition. When wrapping up your work and making the switch back to the mundane world, it helps to pay extra attention to circle unwinding, removing ritual garb, and so on, Eating, bathing, or exercising are also good delineators and can be used before or after the ritual, depending on where they work better for you.

## Humble Pie

When we move our magic out of the Tower and begin processing more of the Data Stream, we gradually begin to appreciate the limitations of other people in general and their perceptions in particular. Discipline, training and practice in any field of endeavor brings about this awareness. It may even dawn on us that the limitations of others can and do have an adverse impact. Once this enters our awareness it is tempting to feel superior to, or be offended by, the apparent stupidity of others.

## Enter Arrogance. Stage Left.

Once it makes its grand entrance, arrogance infects the Data Stream and makes our magic limited and inflexible. Why? The implication of this arrogance is that our worldview is right, superior, or the only path. This is not true. On average we are as ignorant as any other person, only differing in our use of magic and comprehension of the magical worldview. A higher level of awareness applies to many things, not just magic. It applies to ditch digging, accounting, computers, music, philosophy, and the entire range of human endeavor. Our perspective is what counts, not what we look at. With the right attitude anyone can achieve a higher state of awareness, consciousness, and well-being. How they get there is secondary. Where they are going is tertiary. Integration is a key element in avoiding the danger of arrogance. We cannot integrate something if we consider ourselves above it.

Lastly, consider that there are some in the world who would object to our worldview and the impact that worldview has. Even worse, we are not perfect and commit these same errors of ignorance, selfishness, and stupidity that others commit. Hopefully, we know that being a magician does not make us somehow better, or lessen our inaccuracies in some fashion, and instead focus on integrating our weaknesses and making fewer mistakes than others. Note that making fewer mistakes does not make us a better person. It makes us different, possibly more accurate. No more, no less.

## Validation

All too often we seek titles, awards, religion and more to prove that we are right, good and worthwhile. These are good to have but do not bestow rightness, goodness, or superiority. They do highlight the human need for validation. Let's face it. We need support from others. We need to know what we are doing is useful and good for us. We need encouragement, and sometimes a bit of discouragement, to keep ourselves in line and on task.

To keep our need for validation in its proper place, we first look inside and then to the outer world for validation. This requires the most from us because we accept full responsibility for our life and actions. There is no one else to blame. This eliminates a subtle and damaging drain on our magical practice. It eliminates the energy we spend asking for *unnecessary* approval and recognition from others. There is also *necessary* approval, too, because a complete rejection of outside validation, whether from another person or from Reality itself, is not helpful. We cannot ignore the world around us and hope to be effective. We have to work with Reality to ensure we are acting in accordance with it and the inhabitants in it.

# Chapter Five: Back to Mystery School

I started my magical career as a solitary practitioner and it was probably for the best. On the positive side, I learned basic skills and Reality Paradigms on my own terms. Furthermore, the effects of a group's Consensus Reality never had a chance to adversely shape me in ways that were limiting. In hindsight, I also see the negative side — an over-inflated sense of Self and a distinct lack of perspective on the subject. Now that I do lots of group work (mostly non-magical), I can compare and contrast the two methods and get an understanding of groupthink, egregores, and other memes that come into play when people get together.

It's easy to find reasons to avoid joining a local magical Order, coven, secular club, or mystery school. For starters, it takes commitment and hard work. In the case of secular organizations, our reticence may come from the fringe status we find ourselves relegated to because we *practice magic* (say those last two words in a mortified stage whisper). The sheer difficulty of getting over the average person's prejudices and preconceived notions is enough to make us tuck our cape between our legs, run straight into our Tower, lock the door and never ever come out again. The good news is that the prejudice can be avoided. It's simple. We keep our mouths shut. Average folks care about as much about our magical leanings as they do about whether we attend church on Sunday. Most don't give a rat's ass, and the ones that do are usually people we don't want to know anyways.

Whether secular or magical, this kind of work is a valuable aid to our development as people. We have the opportunity to learn things like organizational skills, speaking skills, leadership skills, and social skills with people who want to see us succeed. Good organizations generally recognize that if we are successful, then the group is successful, and everybody wins. Great ones actively seek to create those circumstances.

It might be best that the first group you join be a distinctly secular organization. As a general rule, they are a bit more impervious to the problems religious and magical organizations have. In the context of group work, Magical Orders might also be valid avenues, but only if they have a local chapter where you can get a fairly consistent amount of face time. This also assumes the group in question isn't way out in la-la land.

Groups by definition and purpose have cult-like characteristics. It's unavoidable. Magical groups in particular seem to fall prey to cult and ego issues. Actually, all groups are prone to these problems. Some have better coping mechanisms than others. Working in a healthy organization can give us a feel for the difference between normal group activity and something less desirable. We can also cultivate our ability to walk away from an organization that doesn't meet our needs or starts going down the tubes.

One of the coping mechanisms used by different societies, magical or secular, is an oath that "binds" you to the group. You may have an aversion to this because oaths are unnecessary, dangerous, or have some other equally loathsome quality. Fair enough. But individuals working together do better when there is a sense of common ground and a sense of what each member can expect from every other member. Oaths to *each other* are an effective method to accomplish this. Be leery of an oath to *the group*. It's worth pointing out that taking an oath isn't the only way of creating group cohesion. Agreeing to follow a Code of Conduct, bylaws, or rules is pretty much the same thing as taking an oath. However, those options do not carry the modern (and I emphasize the word modern) stigma oaths seem to have gathered about them.

Before rejecting an institution outright because it requires an oath, there are a few points to consider. First, it seems that the concept of "oath" has become intertwined with "religion" and many of us occult types have experienced bad juju with religion. To add insult to injury, oaths *are* serious business. Because of that, time spent thinking about the implications of an oath is time well spent. Personally, I spent over five years dithering about whether I should join an organization that required an oath. I don't regret joining, but your circumstances may dictate a different course of action.

Oaths have power because they are a statement of intent as powerful as any spell. Part of this power comes from the *limitations* an oath creates. However, these limitations are not always a removal of certain things from our life. In a personal conversation with Scarlett Sankey, writer, friend, and occultist (2007), we decided that, in fact, an oath is a narrow threshold that, once passed over, opens up a different range of action and possibility.

A particular type of occult society, the mystery school, made use of oaths extensively. These schools, or initiatory traditions, taught their pupils by having the initiate actively experience and take part in the lessons. In many cases the lessons were secret, hence the oaths. The teachings consisted of rituals that handed down the symbolic truths of religion, spirituality, morality and virtue a particular school taught. Many were divided into degrees and intended to open the initiate to higher levels of consciousness as they progressed. In many cases, the experience left their participants profoundly changed.

The mystery schools, whether they said so or not, were predicated on the student achieving gnosis (the classic kind, not the Chaos kind). Gnosis to the average Joe tends to mean "knowledge." However, in mystery school terms, gnosis was something that could only be learned through experience. It wasn't something that could be taught by normal means. In fact, it is my personal opinion that mystery schools and initiatory traditions were, and are, held together by the bond formed when members share an experience that is difficult to explain to someone who hasn't had the opportunity.

As a general rule, the schools helped the student achieve gnosis via an initiation cycle that led the pupil through steps corresponding to the stages of life: birth, coming of age, death, and rebirth. The underlying intent seemed to be that until we were "reborn" into a new consciousness, and left our old way of life behind, we weren't going to understand the hidden mysteries of life. Obviously, your mileage may vary. There are plenty of examples of old Mystery Schools, their organization, effects on initiates, and intent presented by Leadbeater (1998) and Hall (2003).

Symbolically, being initiated into a mystery school is a real world enactment of our willingness to tap into a particular egregore. Whether that egregore is the power of the group or something larger probably depends on the group in question. However, the energy is there and useful for us to progress upon the path the group follows and encourages. In fact, that egregorial power is there in purely secular organizations, too. It's also called momentum.

Whether or not group membership is ultimately for you is your decision. Should you decide to go mystery school shopping, look for a tendency towards inclusiveness instead of exclusiveness. In other words, favor organizations that don't require you to be a particular race, color, or religion. This doesn't mean that there aren't certain requirements, but those requirements aren't intended to be onerous. There are some Masonic Orders open to women and/or men, but traditional Freemasons require a belief in deity and a penis. The druidic Ár nDraíocht Féin requires you to be pagan, some Rosicrucian Orders require you to be Christian, the Order of Bards, Ovates, and Druids has few requirements, and most Golden Dawn groups are fairly light on their requirements to join.

At this point, you may be thinking about forming your own group. There's a lot that goes into making a group viable, successful and long lived. It's a lot more than a few paragraphs from me can cover. My advice is to join one first and learn the ropes from those with experience. There's an amazing amount of leadership, organizational and social skills that can be learned. Those are the skills that make a group successful.

The length of time needed to acquire this knowledge varies, but a good rule of thumb is to participate until you are given a leadership position. Thirty years ago, that might have taken a decade. These days, with membership numbers dwindling in most fraternal organizations, it might take anywhere from two to five years. In magically oriented groups, it may take you a year or two to get there. Magical groups can be notoriously deficient in the skills you need to build a thriving organization of your own. My two cents... stick with your granddad's (or grandma's) social fraternity. Those old codgers know their business.

If groups aren't for you but you'd like to get a feel for the initiation cycle mystery schools use to impart gnosis, I've provided an initiation cycle that you can read through or perform on your own to experience and experiment with the effects. It goes through the cycle of birth, coming of age, death, and rebirth.

## Mystery School

I begin by taking a bath by the light of a single candle. This calms and relaxes me. When I'm done, I dress in clean clothes go to my ritual area, taking the candle with me. I place it in the East. Standing in the center I walk a figure 8 while humming to myself. I stop in the middle and sit down with my knees to my chest facing the single candle.

Recollections of the bath, water and comforting darkness arise. Before me I see a dark tunnel and I enter. The candle is the light at the end of the tunnel. I move towards the light. I reach this gateway and stand on the threshold a moment. I step through.

I'm in a bright and sunny glade and a new world. I've willingly chosen the path of the magician. I am awake!

I form a circle by walking the perimeter of the glade. In the center of this enchanted space a mighty tower forms. Two dragons guard the entrance. I attempt to enter. I am not allowed to pass. To the left side of the entry are a hood and some rope. To proceed I must do so in darkness and by mine own hand. This I do willingly. And so I choose darkness.

Hands lead me. I sense torchlight and the presence of unknown others in a great room. A gong resonates thrice. Energy rises as a circle is cast and a disembodied voice calls the forth the quarters of Earth, Air, Fire, and Water!

I come here of my own free Will with open mind and heart yet a voice responds, "Lo, what is this? A blind and bound candidate? Why is this?"

I have freely chosen darkness and bondage.

"Then you have not achieved free Will. You come with open mind and eyes to see, but you do not yet ken what you view. We cannot make this aright. As you have chosen darkness and bondage, so can you choose light and freedom."

"Do you?"

"Do you?"

"Do you?"

I nod my assent to be answered with, "Why?"

Fully, honestly and completely I give my answer.

"Free yourself, for we cannot help."

All others have left.

I am alone in the center of a chamber in the tower. Blind and bound. I struggle with my hood, my ropes and my fears. The struggle only tightens my bonds. Imprisoned by mine own choice, by fetters I myself placed upon my being. Yet, calm prevails. My mind clears. I willingly do this. My limitations I cannot overpower, but perhaps I can integrate and understand them. Awareness shifts. The fetters loosen and fall to the floor. I am free in a room dark but for a single candle at the far end. It beckons me. Hope in darkness.

With newfound freedom comes newfound responsibility. I approach the candle. I am equal in all realms and worlds, free in my choices and lord of my destiny. I reach the candle. I accept that my Will manifests and the responsibility that acceptance implies. I take hold of the candle. I embrace solitude and I embrace society with the declaration that I choose to be a magician. I raise the candle above my head and make myself known by speaking my name. I am known as [name. Yours, preferably]. As I am identified in this world so am I known in all worlds! Torches flare and the chamber radiates light. I return the candle.

*Integration not redemption. Spirals not lines. All experience is subjective. I am a power born of integration on my terms and with my full awareness.*

As the echoing words fade I thank the quarters and dismiss them. Water, Fire, Earth, and Air. I leave the tower. In the glade, the circle unwinds. An owl glides to rest in a nearby apple tree. In my mind it speaks.

*Sight is given. Wisdom for its use comes from without and within. It is but a beginning. Come back often to avoid straying. There are enemies and friends. Learn to exist prosperously with both. Such is the circle. Such is life. The spiritual path is never ending. Do not walk it for the experience or its gifts. Walk it because you can or because you must.*

*Give wisely. Take wisely. Share wisely. Such is my counsel.*

*What is to be seen is there. All is open to the open heart.*

*Thus speaketh the owl.*

I accept my limitations. I am given what I can handle and properly use. No more, no less. Born as human, reborn as magician. Yet again am I born. The spiral continues.

The owl spreads its wings and floats away over my head. I can feel the breath of its silent wings.

My time here is almost finished. I am ready to take my place in this and all worlds.

*I welcome pleasure, wealth, and honor but remain free in my choice to do so.*

*I can be poor, abstain, and suffer and do so willingly for I am lord of my own happiness.*

*I expect nothing from the caprice of fortune and I am brave in the face of its ever-changing nature.*

*I enjoy solitude but also embrace the society of man.*

*I am a child with children, joyous with the young, staid with the old, patient with the foolish, and happy with the wise.*

*I smile with all who smile and mourn with those who weep.*

*I applaud strength and am patient with weakness.*

*I offend no one and have no need to pardon for I never myself feel offended.*

*I respect those who misconceive me and seek opportunity to serve them through example.*

*I can love without being loved and exalt myself above the honors of winning for I possess that which I seek, profound peace.*

*I regret nothing that must end but remember with satisfaction that I have met with the good in all.*

*Hope for me is certainty, for I know that it is eternal.* Adapted from Levi (1974)

The tunnel to my time and place re-opens. The light of my world beckons. I return to the place from where I came. I stand up, extinguish my candle, and complete my journey.

# Chapter Six: Archetype Schmarkytype

I'm a bad toad. On occasion I've said that I hate Harry Pottery and had the temerity to feel justified and smug about it. But, because smugness only goes so far, I decided to figure out why I have such a strong reaction to the guy. I mean, I'm fine with other wizards like Gandalf, Merlin, and Harry Dresden. What's my beef with the Potter kid? With a little introspection, I find that it isn't Harry Potter I hate. What gets my goat is real world magicians trying to make themselves into Potter-esque Wizards and surrounding themselves with a Potter-esque world. It seems to me that this approach is more interested in being the archetype instead of the magician.

Archetypes tap into primal facets of existence and Reality, just like symbols and spells. In fact, an archetype is a form of symbol, just like a rune or pentacle. An archetype holds a vast amount of meaning that extends far beyond the basic shapes our minds give that archetype. Like symbols, archetypes are doorways and conduits for facts and Reality, but they are not the fact or the Reality themselves. The clothes are not the human underneath. From a distance it may look that way, but closer examination reveals the shape the human gives the clothing. Being close up also reveals the way the clothing governs what we see of the person beneath.

As magicians, we work with archetypes extensively. Those archetypes can teach us great things, but I'm not sure we always learn what we are supposed to. When we get caught up in the form we lose sight of the function. The danger in working with archetypes is that instead of using the archetype to highlight aspects of our selves and Reality, we attempt to mold ourselves into the archetype. I think every occultist has trodden this path at least once. I know I have. More than once.

Archetypes are templates. We are human. If we place that template upon our humanity it is not an accurate representation of who we are. It doesn't fit because we have an uncanny (dare I say *tricksterish*?) knack of spilling over the boundaries in some places and not filling them up properly in others. When two or more people come together, they must agree on the Reality that they share. If others don't agree with us, or our take on Reality, we may find ourselves at a disadvantage. If the other person understands the archetype presented, but does not accept our brazen attempt to sell a flawed bill of goods, we're hosed. Especially since they are likely to "respect" our choice enough to laugh at us behind our back instead of to our face.

Personal experience indicates that trying to become the archetype is not advisable. Nor am I entirely sure it can ever meet with success. Working with an archetype to help get in touch oneself is significantly different than working to become the archetype at the expense of Self. We are people, not archetypes. Those great and wondrous characters are pure symbolic essence. They are what we might be if we weren't human. There are many definitions for human and humanity. Whatever definition we choose, the fact remains that *we are human*. Attempting to become an archetype denies our essential humanity and creates a barrier between Reality and Self.

What are the warning signs that we've moved from archetype as tool into the detrimental state of mimicking the archetype? If the clothes you wear and the personality you present fit like store bought suits, you might be an imposter. If you feel threatened by anyone or anything that denies your essential archetype-ness, you might be an imposter. If you spend more time reinforcing tried and true archetypical traits than you do on coming to terms with who you really are, you might be an imposter. If, at the end of the day, you have a gut level feeling that you are hiding behind an archetype to avoid Reality, you might be an imposter. If you have a difficult time relating to real people instead of others who choose archetype mimicking, you might be an imposter. If your circle of friends is only in your life because it reinforces your archetype (sometimes colloquially referred to as "The Scene"), you might be an imposter.

There is a better way to advance our cause. Stereotypes. They are a different beastie altogether. Where archetypes tend to deny our humanity, stereotypes by nature embrace it. These personae are generally well established in our culture and working with them is less prone to error because of their familiarity and established boundaries. Knowing the boundaries of Self and stereotype makes it easier to define where we end and a stereotype begins. Our cultural familiarity tends to prevent us from losing perspective when we strike a stereotypical pose because we know we're play-acting. This isn't always true when we attempt to adopt an archetype. Perhaps this is because, when we attempt to adopt an archetype, we get the two confused in our minds?

Whether derived from an archetype or stereotype, there is nothing wrong with using adopted clothing, posture or character traits as leverage to present ourselves a certain way. It's *why* we choose to do it that makes the difference. An honest desire to get to the bottom of our existence and the meaning of our life is to be applauded. We know we've succeeded at integrating (integrating not adopting) parts of an archetype when others refer to us as that archetype without active encouragement on our part. Alternately, we know which archetypes (or stereotypes, for that matter) we most closely align to if an archetype is used to describe us and we never intended to have that particular label.

That being said, I don't feel the task of the magician is to *look* like a magician, prove that I'm a magician, or prove that magic works. The task of a magician is to be effective. Effective magic is improvement of Self and world and when archetypes are used for those purposes then they are used wisely. If used to reinforce what we already know or want to believe then the archetype becomes a stumbling block.

I'm pretty sure I'm about as far from the Wizardly archetype as I can get. But, then again, I'm a money ho in Corporate Babylon and there doesn't seem to be much point in destroying my upward mobility or credibility. In fact, I find that to be distinctly antimagical. Ironically, if I surround myself with the trappings of the archetype instead of integrating that archetype within my own psyche, I have effectively isolated myself from the world. Magic doesn't work in a vacuum.

But magicians wear robes! Magicians act magical! Magicians are supposed to act different! That's what magicians do! No. It isn't. Except for maybe the "act different" part. But even that should be a natural byproduct of living a magical life and not some misguided need to look like a magician to everybody else on the planet.

Potter's world, and other fantasy worlds, are chock full of magical archetypes. In Potter's world the magic stays hidden because it is outside of the norm. This has parallels to our own world. Many of us keep our magical lifestyle under wraps for various reasons, not the least of which is the desire to avoid prejudice, censure, and retribution by others in our society. In contrast, Tolkien's Gandalf was within the social, political, and theological norms for his world. He may have been on the edge, or walking two worlds at once, he most certainly was not human, but he was not *outside*. There was common ground between himself and Middle Earth. Granted, as an archetype himself, Gandalf had the luxury of not having to look to an archetype for answers. There may be a bit of wisdom in that paradigm, too. Archetypes don't have the answers. We do. Archetypes help us to ask the right questions.

We can't be an archetype, but because we are multi-dimensional people in every sense we can be magicians who don't live by magic alone. Whether magical or mundane, we draw from many disciplines to create a composite way of life. We see magic as a philosophy, a process of self-realization, and a tool to help us realize our potential and manifest Will. We don't see putting on the archetype as the answer to the problem.

## St. Ignatius and the Grey Pilgrim

I suppose that since I've railed about the wrong way to approach an archetype I should present at least one way to work with them. It's not the only way. And, quite honestly, I think the underlying intent of what we do is probably more important than the actual methods and techniques used.

When I was younger, I wanted to be like Gandalf because he could cast spells. As I waxed older I became attracted to his wisdom and his ability to bring out the best in others. I realized that, for a wizard, he did not practice a lot of magic. His true power lay in how he worked with people and the world around him. His leadership abilities, morality, wisdom, and lore were all practical abilities that his contemporaries respected. These were all non-magical skills. Interestingly, the talents the hobbits were most familiar with were his ability with fireworks and smoke rings. These were applied wizardry. To me, this meant that he never used magic for magic's sake but as something to augment the manifestation of his Will. As an Istari, he was under proscriptions that forbade using magic against magic or making decisions for others. This explains his solutions to many of the problems he faced and highlights the ways an oath or dedication can shape and focus the work of any magician's Will.

His innate power when viewed in the context of his lack of spell casting made me curious, so I decided to get to know Gandalf and understand the apparent non-magical qualities I admired so much. To do this, and with some guidance from Israel Regardie (2001), I turned to St. Ignatius (1964). He had a technique that involved putting ourselves in Christ's place and trying to understand what he was thinking and feeling and why he was doing what he was doing. It's apparently quite effective for the faithful, and it is also an ingenious way to learn about an archetype. I resorted to the wisdom of St. Iggy while reading the Lord of The Rings and focusing on Gandalf. What was really magical about Gandalf wasn't turning pinecones into fireballs. (Though that was pretty cool.)

I gleaned the following realizations from my meditations and studies:

* Gandalf did not make decisions for others. He made wise suggestions.
* Gandalf did not touch the ring. He knew his limitations and respected them.
* Other beings were worthy of respect. They were not necessarily his equals. He gave others their due and didn't suffer fools.
* He chided others with plenty of fairness as well as an eye to constructive criticism.
* He understood his, and other people's, perceptions of Reality.
* He truly loved his world.
* People were suspicious of wizards at the best of times.
* A little melodrama never hurt a good story. Timing was everything.
* Giving advice or information was a responsibility not to be taken lightly.
* Having information without revealing the source added to his mystique.
* He was efficient in the communication of information and didn't say something more times than necessary.
* He abhorred rumors. Or at least, he didn't like to act on rumors and treated them as the potentially dangerous and misleading information that they embodied. He spent a lot of time researching leads and corroborating the data he collected.
* The responsibility of being wise and knowledgeable was circumspection, patience, and a desire to build trust.
* He was dead certain when he revealed something. He never guessed. Much of the respect he was given came from the accuracy of his observations, answers, and

suggestions. This highlighted the responsibility he had to the trust others placed in his words, actions, and counsel.

With those points in mind, there are some other tidbits we can take from the study of the Wizard. At a distance a Wizard is a figure of great knowledge and power. Sometimes their demeanor is unsettling. Wizards help those who are looking to find what they are looking for. Sometimes, when there is a quest afoot, they lend a helping hand even though they know that what is sought may be painful to realize or accomplish. They do not do this out of malice, but out of awareness that all seekers sometimes need to find things out for themselves. They know that the path to enlightenment is not easy, nor a cure all, nor an end. They know that we must all travel the path more or less alone. Yet they find a way to provide to the traveler the knowledge and support needed to continue on the journey without getting lost. In many cases, particularly in myth, Wizards help non-Wizards because enlightenment comes in many forms and is not limited to someone on a magical path.

A Wizard in myth is generally tied to another archetype, the Seeker who becomes either Warrior or Wizard. The relationship between these two archetypes has deep meaning, which can be tapped to help us become better magicians. We work with the Seeker because of that archetype's strong resonance with the hidden occult meanings of the Wizard. Generally, the Seeker is a younger and/or less experienced person with potential that highlights the Wizard's established, wise, and capable traits.

Rarely in these stories do we read of a Wizard touting their credentials or attempting to prove anything to the Seeker or anyone else. Inevitably, the Wizard is identified with some greater purpose that guides the Seeker's quest. This identification with a greater purpose implies that the Wizard is self-realized. Realization can be many things to many people. One can be realized and not be a Wizard. Lots of people fit that mold — mom, dad, grandparents, sisters, brothers, teachers, and friends. These are the people that have walked the path and who are willing to show us the path. Like the Wizard, they know they can't walk it for us, except possibly a short way to get us started in the right direction.

What exactly does it mean to be realized? Words like transformation, self-improvement, or self-awareness come to mind. As a realized person, a Wizard's goals generally encompass the ongoing task of making themselves better and thereby making their friends and world better. The term realized also implies that a Wizard, as a general rule, knows why they are here, what they are doing and the right way to go about it. Because the realized Wizard knows these things, and cares about themselves and their world, they are willing to help the Seekers to walk the Path. Sometimes they even show Seekers the Path when the Seeker isn't aware of its existence.

If the Wizard represents self-realization then, by taking the first steps and putting those principles into action, the Seeker represents the external application of those principles. The Seeker is sometimes a person desiring to learn and at other times entirely unaware of their potential. Occasionally the Seeker is someone caught up in events well beyond their skills or control. In all cases, they rely (willingly or unwillingly) on the Wizard until they develop to the point where they can finish the task they started, or were forced to start, on their own. Generally, as the Seeker becomes who they truly are the Wizard fades further into the background.

There is a very important occult principle at work here. Especially when one considers the Wizard and Warrior as internal and external faces of the same person. The Wizard symbolizes the internal wisdom, knowledge, and transformation that give action purpose. However, it takes a certain amount of ego decompression and humility to be a good Wizard. Being humble allows the Wizard to help Seekers arrive at their own conclusions, make their own decisions, and become who they are. It allows the Wizard to do so without forcing the Seeker to think/act/be a certain way. This can be a problem because lack of ego and strong presence of humility may stay a Wizard's hand from acting for or against any given situation. (A Wizard is humble enough to know that they don't know everything and that it is not inherently right to impose their interpretation of how the world should be on others.) This is where the Seeker comes in.

The Seeker represents the application of the Wizard's transformation in the outer world. The Seeker as Warrior is strong enough, possibly brash enough, and confident enough to actually do what they think is right. The Seeker is willing to challenge the humility of the Wizard and do what it takes to make their world a better place. The Seeker implements externally what the Wizard has realized internally and the Wizard's internal process of realization governs how the Seeker acts.

As the Wizard helps to guide the Seeker in their brashness, so too that very brashness enlivens the Wizard to be, do, act and make themselves and their world a better place. This relationship between these two gives the internal journey of transcendence an external manifestation of that journey.

To varying degrees, we are both Seeker and Wizard. As such, it is incumbent upon us to push the boundaries of what we know and who we are. To poke and prod ourselves into really thinking about whom we are and what we want to be. Working with an archetype is one method for doing that. Quite honestly, the only wrong way to deal with an archetype, or anything for that matter, is to use it to stay snuggled in our belief system and insulated from the world at large.

# Chapter Seven: Principia Pokera

Hear ye! Hear ye! Let the magician understand how magic works by cogitating, thinking and otherwise pondering upon the card game of Poker. Compare and contrast magic with a card game and gain insight into how life really works. Er, maybe not. But if ubermensa magician Crowley can make play of finding esoteric wisdom in nursery rhymes, surely the Principia Pokera has its place in esoteric canon?

### Ace of Clubs

The Laws of Chance and Averages govern poker. Statistically speaking, if eight people played poker for a decade, the winning average amongst all 8 players would be the same. Therefore, being a successful poker player isn't about winning hands, it is about winning money.

### Two of Diamonds

To win money, a good poker player must understand the odds, the rules of the game they are playing, and the people they are playing with. Said player knows when odds are favorable to play for a win as well as when they are at a disadvantage and should minimize their losses. Basically, an effective poker player knows when attempting to apply and manifest their Will has the best chance for success.

### Three of Hearts

This is also true for a magician. The laws of magic are there, understood by few, and understood perfectly by none. The magician works with odds, with momentum, and with their Will to maximize what they want from a situation. Playing every hand in poker is akin to a magician casting a spell for every event in their life. It is a waste of energy for the magician and money for the card player. In fact, successful Poker players fold (don't play a hand and relinquish their stake in the winnings) many more times than they play.

### Four of Spades

In poker, money is momentum. You can afford to make mistakes or take chances when you have the big stack of chips. You can use your momentum to force others out of the hand and thereby win a hand you might not normally play. When you are short stacked (low on chips), you must husband your resources and make them count.

### Full Boat

A poker player must know their opponents. A magician must understand the people they interact with. A poker player needs to have a good idea of what reaction may be created by their actions. This is the same for the magician.

### Deuces Wild

A card sharp gains nothing by giving other people information about what they are doing or their capabilities. Ditto the magician. By telling another everything you know, intend to do, or are capable of doing, you subject yourself to their influence. In poker, this is devastating. In real life, it can have the same consequences.

### Straight Flush

A skilled poker player isn't as effective when another good poker player is at the table. When you have two people vying to win at poker, only one can win, no matter how much skill they apply. Magicians are subject to a similar dynamic. They are more likely to find common ground and work in harmony…but not always. It is quite possible that you may find yourself working against another magician's Will. Not in some "I win, you lose" capacity, but in that ordinary way people have of running counter to another's intentions while not actively intending to be detrimental to each other.

### Aces and Eights

Magicians and poker players must be able to adapt to their environment. In poker, no two games are alike. Different players create different environments. Some are easier than others for the player to work with. This is the same for the magician.

## Ante Up

Learning to play poker has parallels to learning anything. You must learn the basics and then learn to apply them. Then you must learn enough to know what questions to ask and what information you need to help yourself improve. Experience counts in both disciplines. The more you know, the better you can apply the knowledge. Magicians and poker players both know that they have to be able to analyze their game and improve upon it. Both know that improvement takes time, keeping track, and more than their fair share of losing.

## Bob's Your Uncle

There are poker players and magicians who talk the talk and cannot walk the walk. Only results speak at a poker table, in real life, and in magical practice. As a magician, or poker player, you learn what you can from these people and respect them for who they are. In both poker and magic there are naturals who don't know all the technical or historical minutia of the discipline. They are still good at what they do. Egalitarianism might satisfy ones ego, but is worthless if no one else buys what you are selling.

## Plums are Tall

From the standpoint of poker as a practical magical exercise, poker is a great environment for a magician to develop their Will. You want to win; your opponents want you to lose. Like it or not, this affects your play. The more you play, the better you get at isolating your Will from the impact of another's Will and the more likely you are to make decisions in accord with your Will. This has parallels with your interaction with others. In games of chance or real life, situations where the rules are not completely understood tend to even out the odds and skill becomes a deciding factor more often than not. But, like life, skill isn't always the deciding factor.

## Dealer Calls

Different kinds of poker, such as Seven Card Stud, Texas Hold 'Em, and Omaha have parallels to different magical systems. In poker, these are ways to interact with 52 cards, how they are dealt, how they are bet on, and how they manifest the universal laws of odds. Magical systems are the same. They are ways to interact with magic/life, but they are not magic/life. In other words, the chosen magic "system" governs how you interact with magic, but it does not change the magic itself. It merely highlights different aspects of the root concept.

Thus ends *Principia Pokera. Bake it in the oven for baby and me!*

# Chapter 8: The Obligatory Grimoire

Most Grimoires are a magician's collection of spells and magical methods. This chapter is no different. It's a collection of ideas, techniques observations and bric-a-brac that I've not found elsewhere, or at least not many elsewheres, and implemented in my own magical practice. Take 'em or leave 'em, I hope you find the ideas stimulating and enjoyable.

## Pentacle of Perception

The Pentacle of Perception is a framework that helps us implement magical thinking in our lives. It helps us understand how we work with information and come to terms with our thought processes. It teaches the stages of paying attention, knowing something, integrating it, and then transforming ourselves. It also helps address the modern tendency to consume information, or our life experiences, as if these things were disposable objects. We can use the Pentacle to move right on past where most people stop and onto the end result of Transformation. Transformation is a holistic attempt to properly implement the Hermetic Axiom of "As Above, So Below."

The Pentacle is useful for addressing the fact that there is no requirement that we understand our Will or comprehend the implications of our actions. Our Will, especially when distilled by magic, manifests even if we are unprepared for the results. By nature it does not take the "why" into account and focuses solely on the "what." At best, this means we manifest Will with no internal integration whatsoever (I'd like fries with that). At worst, we experience integration we are not aware of or in control of at any level (Ding! Fries are done). With this Pentacle, we may prevent these things from happening to us.

The Pentacle can also help lay a solid foundation for making accurate snap decisions. Life, being life, likes to create situations that demand we act quickly and without the benefit of reasoned review. In many of these situations we can take a moment to open ourselves to the underlying concepts of the Pentacle and get a visceral awareness of the implications of our actions. At the very least, this act of "opening up" indicates a willingness to accept responsibility for our choice and the results. In extreme circumstances, when a split second decision is required, we hope that our Tower work to date, in tandem with the Pentacle, provides us with a foundation to instinctively make the right choice.

The five steps of the Pentacle are presented as distinct phases of a process but, in reality, there is a subtle interplay between each of the five points and no point is isolated from the others. How these concepts intertwine and create a powerful transformative process becomes clearer as we work with this paradigm. We follow this discussion with a presentation on how the Pentacle can be used to integrate magic and Reality as a composite whole. These five steps are inspired by ideas presented in a series of pamphlets on mnemonic memory by Clark (1920). His intent was to show how to use the process of learning to help the process of memorization, but with some arm-twisting the process works exceptionally well for how we work with information in general.

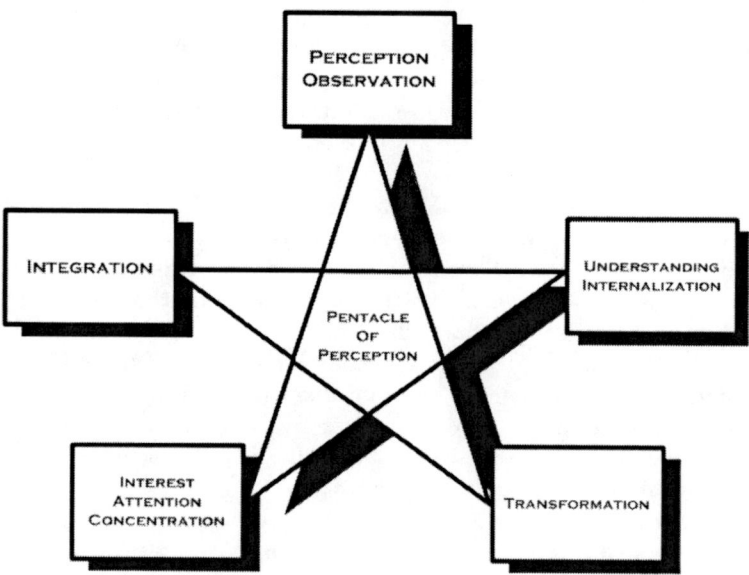

### 1. Perception and Observation

Without the ability to perceive and observe we have no information to work with. We must first become aware that something exists, or can potentially exist, to create opportunities to work with it. Perception and Observation are the first steps for tapping into the Data Stream. We view life through filters that control what we see and choose to observe. To expand upon what we perceive, there are three tasks for the magician at this initial stage. The first is to become aware of the filters, or box, through which we interact with life. The next task is to broaden the limits of our box. By expanding these limits we perceive and observe more of the life happening around us. Our final and ongoing task is to maintain an awareness of our filtered limits and work with life accordingly.

## 2. Interest, Attention, and Concentration

After we become aware of something, it must hold our interest. If we perceive and observe something and decide that it isn't worth taking note of, then we then discard that information. The filters of ignorance and disinterest keep a lot of information at bay. These filters are necessary because it is utterly impossible for us to work with every bit of information we have access to. The Pentacle is intended to help us find a balance between trying to work with everything and working with the parts of the Data Stream we find useful. When something does catch our interest, it engages our attention. Attention is a deepening of our initial interest and signifies a commitment on our part to retain what we have learned for further consideration.

Once something has our attention we concentrate upon it. The act of concentrating can be divided into two categories. The first is a narrowing of our field of perception to a single idea or fact. The second is a widening of our view in an attempt to encompass the whole. In the first, or focused, instance we increase our ability to gain information about a particular thing while decreasing new input about anything else. In the second, or diffused, instance we concentrate on getting as much information as possible by loosely holding the concept in our mind and opening up to as many related associations as we can find. Once we have enough information, we can then take the further step of concentrating on aspects of that information by using the focused method.

In essence, concentration can be used to change the perspective we use to interact with an object. This state of mind is achieved in numerous ways. Meditation, ritual, focusing on only one of the five senses, personifying an object, and viewing something within the context of a single Rune are all methods that come to mind. Like changing out the lens in a stage light, these activities affect how we view something. By proactively using our built-in filters to highlight different facets of an idea, we gain new information about any given object.

## 3. Understanding and Internalization

With Understanding we become familiar with and make sense of a particular idea. There isn't anything particularly fancy about it. This is the ordinary, garden-variety phase of learning as we know it. Unfortunately, most people stop here because they don't see acquiring knowledge as part of a larger holistic process of Integration and Transformation. When we stop at Understanding, this process becomes a consumption of data. It is akin to buying a book, reading the Table of Contents, then putting the book on a shelf and assuming we know all we need to about that subject. The person who controls this information misses out on a completely different plane of understanding and they confuse Wisdom with Knowledge. As magicians we can take this a step (well, a couple of steps) further and Internalize our knowledge.

Internalization is the voluntary act of "taking possession" of an idea and making it our own. It is at this stage we begin to truly interact with an idea. Think about your pet theories, philosophies, and ideas on subjects familiar to you. You don't view these as external to yourself. They are a part of you and contain bits of your life experience. This is what it means to Internalize information. You take ownership, and by extension responsibility, for the data.

## 4. Integration

Integration takes what we started in the previous step and makes an idea a contributing part of ourselves. Once internalized, an idea it achieves equal footing with things we already know. We are now in a position to integrate the idea. If we do not give an idea equal footing then that idea is subject to control by us. Control may be necessary at times, but control of an idea is not Integration.

Integration implies control but is not control. We can control a lot of things but they are not necessarily integrated. This is because integration requires humility. To integrate an experience we cannot consider ourselves better than the experience. We must be of the mind that we do not know everything and can never know everything. Information is infinite and consciousness is finite. To make things difficult, we must also be able to integrate an experience without becoming the experience.

Magical integration entails improving upon an experience we've had by giving something back to it as we take something useful from it. It means we don't consume the experience as if it were a commodity to be used and thrown away. The experience is something that becomes a useful part of our life. For example, in the case of a bad experience, the Integration can take the form of not making the same mistake again or bringing as much positive knowledge as we can from a particular event. Giving back might take the form of personifying the experience and interacting with it so that we can learn from it and it can learn from us.

Integration is also an ongoing process that is never quite done. This is reflected every time we talk with a friend about a subject important to us. We return to ideas, add to them, subtract from them, understand them better, and possibly reject them entirely at some later date. It is something we've always done. Using the Pentacle to observe and regulate the process gives us a new tool to work with the Data Stream.

Once integrated, an idea has the opportunity to transform us via the creation of new ideas and associations within ourselves. We introduce existing ideas to each other, nurture the relationship, and watch as these ideas form new relationships within our awareness. Integration and Transformation are closely linked.

## 5. Transformation

Transformation is the final step of the Pentacle of Perception. It is the threshold where an idea becomes something more than the sum of its parts. Transformation makes an idea an active growing thing that continues to add to our inner world. It opens us to new opportunities by returning again to the first step, Perception... but perception at a higher level than where we started.

But what is Transformation? Transformation is difficult to describe. It can be a seed thought, phrase, or emotion that spawns a poem. It can be an unpredictable threefold process: the reading, doing, or experiencing of one thing. Then, while reading, doing or experiencing another thing, a third experience, action, or thought is born. This third thing is separate and unrelated to the first two, yet inspired and created by both.

Transformation can be that almost indescribable feeling we get when we know in our heart we have discovered yet another piece of "the puzzle" through meditation, ritual, or good old fashioned life experience. Transformation is sometimes that dark, gaping part of our Inner Self that we don't quite understand.

Transformation knows that someday we can understand. Transformation may humble us to the utmost. Transformation may exhilarate us beyond words. It is a part of who we are.

## The Pentacle of Perception in Action

To come to terms with how we work with information by using the Pentacle as a vehicle for self-transformation, let's take a look at Nigel Pennick's (1998) method for creating a runic talisman. We begin by creating or selecting a talisman. Once that is done, the talisman is placed in a symbolic womb and allowed to symbolically "gestate." Then it is "birthed" by naming it and identifying its purpose. Finally, it is released into the world to fulfill that purpose. This symbolic procreative process of seeding, gestation, birth, and life ensures that we take each step in the right order and in the right manner. In essence, we ensure that we take responsibility for our actions by approaching that action as a child of our creation. These steps map to the Pentacle in the following way:

*Perception and Observation.*

We've identified something that needs to change and decided to act on that information.

*Interest, Attention, and Concentration*

We decide on what talisman to construct and create it. By doing so, we apply your concentration and attention to the matter at hand. Obliquely we are addressing our intended course of action by selecting a symbolic representation of what it is we wish to happen.

*Internalization and Understanding*

By conducting our rite we indicate we are ready to move forward and act upon the information. By placing the talisman in the symbolic womb, we symbolize the act of Internalization. By naming the talisman and giving it the task for which it was born, we indicate our Understanding of what needs to be done.

*Integration*

Furthermore, as the symbol is birthed, we symbolically enact the process of integration. We are the parent. By choice, this sigil is a part of us and our Reality, for good or ill.

## Transformation

Transformation is both the beginning and end result of this process. It is the end in the sense that we have completed the steps necessary to bring our talisman to life. It is the beginning in the sense that the talisman is now functional. At this point, we have moved ourselves beyond an initial awareness of the situation, indicated our intention to act upon it, and symbolically enacted our intent. Now we work to realize our intention by completing the transformative process of Self and world. In effect, we are transforming Reality much the same way we transform our Inner World by creating a "Eureka!" moment... or at least, creating conditions favorable for the "Eureka!" moment.

## Goal Setting and the Eight Festivals of the Year

*"No goal can be accomplished by magic alone. Nor can a magician be successful with only magical goals."*

Many sages, wizards, and magician have stated that phrase using a myriad of words and languages. One of the simplest variations is *"Faith without works is dead, Jim."* In essence, magic is only one tool we use to manifest Will. We must balance magic with other means. Goals provide us with that balance and they move nebulous ideas of what we want to accomplish into the concrete structure of goal setting. They also help to prevent overdependence on magic by identifying ways in which we can achieve our objectives that don't require a spell for every step of the process.

As magicians we push the envelope of living consciously *and* conscientiously because we know that using magic makes us magicians. No more, no less. Magic is not the end result. *Results* are the true measure of magical success. We are successful when the result is an expansion of who we are and not a protective skin used to shelter us from the demands of Reality. Magic isn't here to keep us safe.

Goals teach us how to use magic in a positive manner. Without them we can easily make the mistake of identifying who we are with the magic instead of the result. Focusing on goals relieves us of the temptation to "prove" our magic when there is generally no (objective) proof. When we successfully use magic to achieve goals, we aren't worried about how well we do the spell or how much arcane knowledge we drag up to make a more powerful spell. Our primary concern and sense of pride is being a successful person.

It is essential to balance our magical development in the Tower by applying ourselves in the real world. This forces us to compete in an arena where participants bring all their tools, tricks, knowledge, and wisdom to the contest. Some of the most realized people in the world have no truck with magic. Yet, they can still be thought of as successful magicians who deserve respect because they have manifested Will in a way that expands who they are. After all, it is very easy to cast a *Hell-Bent-For-Leather-Goddess-Come-Hither Spell* ™, but getting our dream job takes work. If being successful at magic becomes more important than developing all aspects of who we are, we may spend precious time and energy using magic to prove what good magicians we are instead of getting results.

Goals are the difference between spending one hundred dollars worth of Will without another thought or creating a budget that specifies where we want the hundred dollars to go (and then following through on that budget, of course). We balance the inner work of self-improvement with the outer work of *doing something useful* with that improvement.

Achieving a goal creates a positive feedback loop. When we achieve what we put our minds to, we have more faith in our ability to manifest Will. This makes it easier to accomplish the next task, and so on. Goal setting also has more to it than achieving something. It can also be used to teach us the mechanics of being a successful person.

It is entirely possible that ancient ceremonial magicians were required to make a sword (and other magical implements) for reasons beyond creating some mystical magical link between the magician and the implement. (Not that this was a bad thing.) The requirement may have also been put in place to force the would-be magician to learn not just a set of skills, but "how to learn." The process of taking iron ore from the ground, smelting it, forging it, and finishing it into a blade is an involved process. Learning how to do something like that is a worthy magical achievement because, if we are paying attention, we are learning a subset of skills geared around asking questions, working with people, finding resources, acquiring knowledge and then putting our acquired knowledge into action. That subset of skills can be used to great effect in other areas of our life, say... like... achieving goals (Imagine that.).

Properly working with goals can be done in many ways. If

you already have a method that you use, by all means continue to use it. Read through this information and consider some of the deeper symbolic and esoteric aspects of the material, but don't feel as though you must switch methods or construct a hulking 80-pound claymore broadsword. This chapter teaches goal setting using the seasonal cycle of equinoxes, solstices, and cross quarter Festivals. If you do create that monster sword, I want to see it. From a safe distance. If you please.

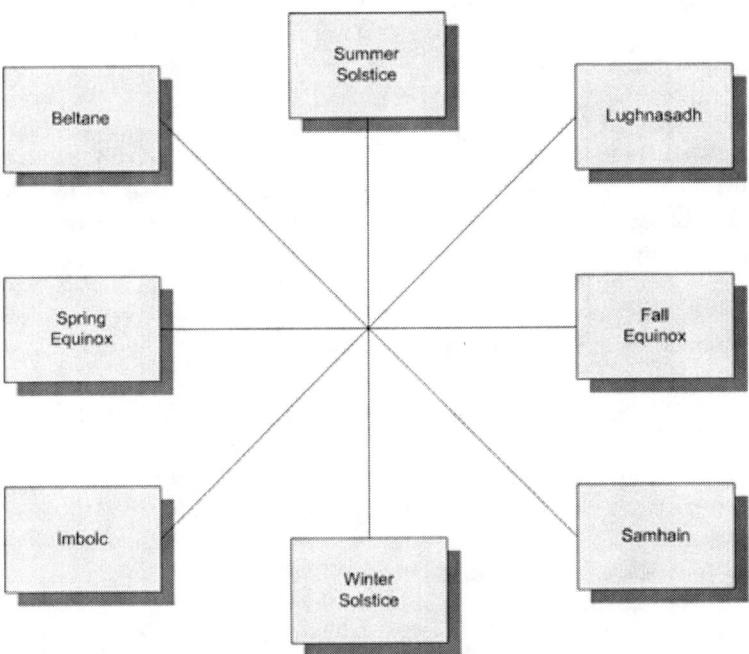

The Equinoxes and Solstices mark the calendar beginnings of Spring, Summer, Autumn, and Winter. Like a magical alphabet, this progression has, through myth and legend, acquired deep symbolic meaning. Using agriculture as an example, Spring is the time of planting, Summer the time of Growing, Autumn the time of Harvest, and Winter the time the fields lie fallow until the cycle begins again. By working with the Festivals we add extra symbolic depth to our goals and the way we celebrate achieving them.

There are many sources and interpretations of the number and character of seasonal Festivals. For our purposes I've adopted more or less modern neo-Celtic interpretations and referenced both King (1999) and McCoy (1995) when in doubt. Let's take a look at these eight seasonal Festivals, starting with Imbolc. (Note that each section starts with the name of the Festival, its approximate date, and the corresponding point on the Pentacle of Perception.)

## Imbolc, February 2nd: Perception and Observation

Imbolc celebrates and marks the turning point of winter. During this season, ewes give birth to their first lambs and the earth begins to show sporadic signs of the coming Spring. It is a time of new beginnings and hope.

Thinking of Imbolc in terms of the Western "New Year" and its goal setting customs gives us an idea of how to approach this holiday. It is a time to review the past year, celebrate what the future has in store for us, set new goals, and open ourselves to new possibilities. During Imbolc, we choose which goals we wish to pursue and make a pact to pursue those goals.

Imbolc ties to Perception and Observation in the Pentacle of Perception because we have chosen to "perceive" a course of action and package that perception as a Goal.

## Spring Equinox, March 21st: Preparation/Planning

The Spring Equinox marks the plowing and sowing of fields. Winter eases its grip on the land and we make ready for the year to come. This Festival is the time to actively plan and prepare to achieve a goal by mapping out the steps we feel are necessary to get from beginning to end. It's like plowing the field in a straight line so the seeds take hold. We plant our seeds and take the first steps in realizing our goals. This planting forms the foundation of our goals and the harvest to come.

Before planting our seeds, however, we must prepare the field by clearing away debris, plowing the soil, and making repairs to any damage caused by Winter. In essence, it is time for "Spring Cleaning" and we take the time to ensure that we can pursue our new goals by clearing out the old and laying the foundation for the new. In a sense, we "clean" our lives by putting aside old goals, hobbies, or habits so that we have room for our new goal to manifest.

This equinox corresponds to Perception and Observation in an active sense. Where Imbolc was the introspective work of goal setting, the Spring Equinox is the actual planting of the seeds.

## Beltane, May 1st: Interest, Attention, and Concentration, or Alternately Action/Execution

Beltane symbolizes the active pursuit of our goals. Beltane is both the decision to act on a goal and acting on that decision. There are many traditions associated with Beltane. The maypole and driving livestock between two fires are primary examples of these traditions. The maypole has male generative or active symbolism, and livestock has overtones of planning and cooperation. Both imply action and fertility. It is the beginning of a year of hard work and diligence that ensures our Spring efforts come to fruition.

This Festival maps to Interest, Attention, and Concentration, but a more accurate moniker might be "Action and Execution" because this process is an external manifestation of the Pentacle. As an idea might wither due to lack of interest, so might a goal never be realized due to lack of action.

## Summer Solstice, June 21st: Internalization and Understanding

Midsummer represents the hard work of tending our herds and crops. Achieving something takes more than wishful thinking. It takes dedication and work. Sometimes that work isn't glorious or fun. Sometimes there are setbacks and delays. The Summer Solstice is the goal setting equivalent of weeding, tending sick cattle, watering the fields, or dealing with the aftermath of violent Summer storms. Yet, as we do these mundane tasks, we improve.

This Festival maps to Internalization and Understanding because sometimes, in the early parts of our goal-setting year, we don't know the cost of a goal. Usually, the true cost of commitment becomes apparent in the Summer when the days become hot and make work drudgery. It is here that we must accept and come to terms with the price of our commitment. By understanding that our final goal means more than just the day-to-day work, our day-to-day work is no longer a chore, but a means to an end.

This is especially true when we realize that we are achieving new levels of skill and understanding through consistently working towards the end result. Yes, the longest day of the year brings hot days and hard work. But it also brings long hours of illumination for those who use the daylight wisely. Our goals may not be realized, but our actions are in full bloom.

## Lughnasad, August 1st: Achievement, Exhibition, Celebration

Lughnasad was a time of games, competition, and other contests of skill. In goal setting, the Festival is a waypoint, and it symbolizes progress to date. During Lughnasad we revel in, celebrate, and demonstrate the knowledge and skill we have acquired working towards our goal. We celebrate, not the achievement of the goal itself, but how far we have come from the seed thought which started our journey. This is a time of reward and recognition for our efforts and represents our desire to show and share them. Granted, we may not feel a need to share this waypoint with anyone but ourselves but, privately or publicly, we do celebrate the journey.

Lughnasad maps to Internalization and Understanding, but it is an external acknowledgement and celebration of our efforts, hence the association with Achievement, Exhibition, and Celebration.

## Fall Equinox, September 21st: Integration

Historically, harvest time was all-important and the entire community participated. Because of this, cooperation was, and is, a watchword for the Fall Equinox. Seasonally, the Fall Equinox marks the beginning of Autumn. The weather, its impact on the growing season and ensuing harvest can serve as symbols of the uncertainties, unknowns and external influences that play a significant part in the process of gathering our crops as well as the yield's quality.

"Reaping what one has sown" is an important motif during this time. We harvest our labors and the results of a good or bad year of work and weather. This is the turning point when our path has moved beyond its beginning and middle and towards the end of the cycle. We have achieved our goal. It is a fact externally as well as internally. Yet, the harvest is not the end of the cycle, whether we consider it agriculturally or in terms of our goals.

This season ties to Integration because it is here that we begin to maximize what we have learned and experienced while attaining our goal.

## Samhain, November 1st: Transformation

Samhain was traditionally the time when the veil between our world and the Otherworld was at its thinnest. Spirits passed freely between the worlds of men and the Otherworld. Samhain was also the time that the Harvest was stored and preserved to help the community make it through the Winter. Every effort was made to maximize what could be stored for later use.

The first allegory, the thinning of the veil, is appropriate because Spirits of the departed symbolize the past. Symbolically, Samhain is a time for review and assessing where we were and how far we've come. It is a time for giving thanks for all that have helped us to this point. But, like peering too long through the veil and reveling in what was at the expense of what is to come, ever looking back can make us lost and unable to turn back to the world of the present and the future.

The second allegory, the storing of the Harvest, is also appropriate. This is an external manifestation of Will because, as Winter comes, we really do reap what we have sown (and stored). This conveys to us that not only must we achieve a goal, but we must also take steps to ensure that we get maximum benefit from it. Furthermore, it implies that immediate consumption of the fruits of labor might leave us close to starving come Spring.

By using the Pentacle of Perception we find that the transformation comes not only by accomplishing our goal, but also by allowing our actions to transform us in such a way that the accomplishment of the goal becomes not an end, but another beginning that leads us to better and greater things. After all, we can't plant next year's crops if we don't save any seeds.

## Winter Solstice December 21st Transformation, New Beginnings

If Samhain is storing the harvest, then the Winter Solstice is surviving on our efforts for good or ill. In ancient times, humankind lived off what was successfully stored and preserved during the harvest months. There was no second chance. This is appropriate symbolism. Now that we have achieved our goal, we must live with the work we put into that goal and the results of realizing that goal. For good or ill, achieving the goal transforms us and creates opportunity for new beginnings.

In a way, Samhain is the backward looking face of transformation and the Winter Solstice is the forward looking face.

Each stands in the doorway of time, on a threshold, one looking forward to a new year and the other glancing back over the experiences of the previous cycle. As the light of the sun fades we internalize all that we have gained, allow it to lie fallow until Spring, and give ourselves time to truly transform our lives via integration. Such is the Janus of transformation.

In the darkness of completion is the bright point of the new cycle of transformation. It is the time of pause, of new birth when the transformations of the cycles past generate the seeds of the cycles to come. This is also the time when the plenty we have received as a result of our efforts is quietly shared with the world around us and ourselves.

## Exercise

Select one or two goals and implement them using the structure of the eight Festivals. Use the Festivals to mark, assess, and celebrate your progress towards the goals you've set. These goals can be simple or complex.

At Imbolc you decide to purchase a home by next Imbolc. This is probably more of a five-year goal, but take it for the example it is. During your seasonal celebration you write your goal down.

At the Spring Equinox, you map out the steps you need to purchase your new home. You might need to repair your current home or curtail certain expenditures to save money for a down payment (Spring Cleaning). You also identify other steps you need to achieve your goal, things like obtaining a real estate agent, researching where you want to live, figuring out how much the move is going to cost and so on (Planting).

At Beltane, you are actively working to repair your home and save money. During your seasonal celebration, you might take note of your progress and celebrate it to date.

At the Summer Solstice you realize that saving money is challenging, if not downright impossible, or the repairs are more difficult than you realized. Maybe other setbacks (Summer storms) have occurred; say a pay cut or new job. Alternately, you may find that the repairs have gone quite well and your other steps in the goal are coming along quite nicely. At this time you might hire your agent and begin looking for your new home.

At Lughnasad, you realize you've learned a lot about home buying. You understand about down payments and the ins and outs of real estate finance. Maybe you give advice to a friend and help them make decisions buying a new home (demonstration of skill and prowess).

At the Autumn Equinox, your house goes on the market. Here you experience the harvest of your preparations and work to date. Your repairs might make your home worth a little more and potential buyers might be more likely to want your current residence. Also, your preparation for the move has you in position to change residence.

You sell your home around Samhain and purchase your new home. You look back at your year and give thanks to everyone and everything that helped you achieve your goal. But you aren't done. You still need to move.

At the Winter Solstice, for good or ill, you've moved into your new home. The move might be smooth or difficult, depending on your preparation and other factors. The home might be perfect, or as time goes on, you may find it needs repairs of its own. It is during this Winter move that you truly reap what you have sown.

## Exercise in Default Settings

This exercise is a thorough programme of Self Assessment. It provides the information necessary to help you decide what things are no longer necessary to your development as a person, what things you already have, and what things you may need.

It starts with an examination of who you are on the outside and quickly moves to who you are on the inside. It is best performed a little at a time. Budget at least thirty minutes a day for performing this Exercise. If possible, spend that time in the same setting or room every day. Make that space a special place apart from your everyday life. As you work with this you may find that some days are very difficult. Other days, you may find that you spend hours writing about what you learn about yourself. Yes. I said "writing." You are supposed to take notes to help facilitate the process.

**Week 1**

Use the first week (or longer) to analyze the information you present in your posture, scents, inflections, mannerisms, words chosen during speech, and your apparent taste in cars, clothes, and music. Judge not only the motives for all the above but also the underlying reasons for your choices.

## Week 2

Make a list of your strengths and your weaknesses. Make notes of your current status in your career, personal life, and your status as a magician. Take notes regarding what you do know and what you don't know. As regards your career, personal life and magician-hood, make a list of your prejudices, preconceived notions, subconscious beliefs, conscious beliefs, and why you believe you do what you do. This technique is loosely based on techniques espoused by Bardon (2007).

## Week 3 and Beyond!

The remaining weeks are for reviewing the lists you have created and notes you have taken. Detect the patterns that indicate Default Settings or those courses of action that will be taken when you apply Will without being aware of these factors. The questions that follow are guidelines to help you through this. Feel free to add to the list as you deem appropriate. Make it a point to find as many questions as you can that apply to your mundane and magical life. You are trying to identify where you are in life, where you are currently going, and what it would take to change direction. A key question that should underlie all you ask is: When you change direction, are you in a position to control which way you end up facing?

## Suggested Questions

Which settings help you?

Which ones hinder?

What can you do to change them?

Is it possible to bypass those settings long enough to achieve a particular goal or outcome?

Where is the momentum in your life?

Is your career on the upswing?

Is it just starting or ending a phase?

*These questions also apply to your personal life:*

Where is your momentum?

Is it family?

Friends?

Somewhere else?

Is that the direction you want it to manifest?

If you were to cast a spell for money, what is the most likely path it will take to manifestation?

A raise at work?

Borrowing money from a friend?

Winning money gambling?

An inheritance from a death in the family?

If you were to cast a love spell (ugh) how would it manifest?

The person of your dreams?

A one-night stand?

A messed up relationship just like the last one?

Something involving a donkey, a wet suit, and a family size jar of Cheez Whiz?

If you were to cast a spell to improve your ability as a magician, how would it manifest?

No improvement?

Will you move in a completely different direction?

Slow but sure?

Quick and dangerous?

What things are you aware of, or possibly even unaware of, that would cause a spell to manifest in a fashion that is:

In direct contradiction to your wishes?

Unexpected?

Exactly what you wanted?

Dangerous or deleterious?

After the spell has manifested, what other things might happen due to the momentum of the spell?

Jealousy from work mates?

An inability to meet career expectations?

A love triangle you weren't prepared for?

A dangerous extension of your abilities as a magician that you can't cope with?

What would it take to rectify these unexpected manifestations of momentum?

Can you follow through after your initial success?

## People Sigil Magic

People Sigil Magic is based on Chaos Sigil Magic. Chaos Sigil Magic works like this: We create a symbol that represents what we want. The sigil is created by, for example, writing what we want in a sentence, then crossing out all duplicate letters, then combining all the remaining letters into a single simple symbol (The Sigil). Then we achieve a state of trance or gnosis, and concentrate solely on the sigil. Once the spell is complete, we let go of the spell and no longer think about the process. This allows the sigil to work unfettered.

This approach assumes two main enemies to successful magic. One is the psychic censor and the other is called subconscious drag. In short, the psychic censor says, "It didn't happen" and subconscious drag says, "It can't happen." When we use a sigil to represent our Will and then focus on that sigil in an altered state of consciousness we bypass the psychic censor. To some degree we also bypass our subconscious drag, but, according to Carroll, Hine and other Chaos practitioners, successful magic is the best antidote to the belief that magic can't happen. When we stop thinking about the sigil after activating it, we put our meddlesome Will in check, as well as its tendency to manifest fear, uncertainty and doubt, thereby removing subconscious drag from the equation. For more than a glib gloss on the subject I recommend Carroll's *Liber Kaos* (1992), *Liber Null and Psychonaut* (1997) and Hine's *Condensed Chaos* (1995). Or you can type "Chaos Magic" into your favorite online search engine and hold onto your hard drive.

People Sigil Magic or PSM, is used like ordinary sigil magic except that we transmit our Will to another person in such a way that they accept it with little or no argument. They may not accept our Will implicitly, but they generally accept the manifestation of our Will as a possibility. PSM works like this: We cast the spell of our choice in the Tower. As long as it highlights the aspects of Will we want to manifest the spell has done its purpose. The spell itself should NOT be something specifically designed to get the recipient of our Will to act in a particular way. In fact, I've found that it is more effective to cast for results that affect a third party known to the recipient and myself.

Once the spell is done, we spend some time with the recipient. As we speak and interact with them, we should imagine that we are sending them the information about our Will and our spell in non-verbal ways. You'll be surprised that as you talk to them, you really do start to feel as though certain seemingly ordinary hand and eye gestures on your part convey information to them in a most extraordinary way. This may take a couple of sessions before you feel that you've adequately conveyed your Will. Then, monitor the situation to determine results.

When I initially started PSM, I didn't notice the parallels between it and Sigil Magic. But, upon examination, I find that other people function as our psychic censor and we function as our subconscious drag. Like those two magical nemeses, what another person does not know doesn't hurt our magical practice. If we can get information about our Will to them, without giving them a chance to object, then we've effectively "inserted the sigil." On a side note, this may be why practitioners both ancient and modern put such an emphasis on the "silent" part of the maxim "To Know, To Dare, To Will, To Be Silent."

## Sacred Space

Your "Sacred Space" is your mental home and the place you begin your meditations and travels on the inner journey of self-discovery. Using whatever method you feel appropriate, enter into a light trance state (for example clearing your mind and breathing rhythmically). Imagine that you step through a doorway into your Sacred Space. (Alternately, you could journey through a tunnel, or walk up (or down) stairs, or go over a bridge. The idea is to create some sense of separation between your regular frame of mind and your Sacred Space.) Your very first visit might be to a blank, featureless area that you then mold into a place that is safe and special for you. This can be a building, a forest, or a boat on the ocean. The important part is to choose somewhere comfortable and meaningful to you and then add new details as you continue to work with this Discipline.

To take this concept further, many traditions use a symbolic framework to create a sense of cohesion when you work with Self and how that Self interacts with Reality. Some use a Tree of Life, others use the Grail Myths. Others use demons and angels, though maybe they don't view them as a vehicle for self-knowledge. In each, there are entities and symbols with which you create and interact. They help you to identify and work with aspects of yourself that are not easily accessible or worked upon directly. This new symbolic structure provides a means to communicate with your internal Self. It also provides the means for your Inner Self to communicate with you in a way that you can understand and act upon. It's like taking an amorphous blob of feelings and memories and experiences and lumping them into a single person, experience, symbol or structure. Once you shoehorn them into something recognizable, you can then work with it in ways that are constructive.

Rather than force you through a series of meditations designed to help you create a certain type of vibe in your Space a Play is presented. Read through it, use the imagery if you'd like or use the ideas behind it to create your own home, home in the brain.

## Pathworking: A Play in Four Parts

*Persons Represented*

The Magician (that would be you)

The Wizard (somebody not you)

Wise Woman (also not you)

Dwarves (definitely not you)

Elves (most definitely not you)

The Orator (somebody also not you, here to give helpful bits as needed.)

Various Magical Denizens

Act I

Scene 1 – Your Sacred Space

*Enter Orator, who stands Center Stage in your Sacred Space illuminated by a single spotlight.*

Orator: The Magician (that would be you) takes time to ponder upon the kind of house that is appealing and magical. For here dwells a mighty Wizard!

*Exit Orator.*

*Some time later the Magician enters and begins exploring the stage of the Sacred Space. He chants a magical summoning. Cue lights, fog, and other magical type stuff that happens in response to the chant.*

*Enter Dwarves.*

Dwarf Leader: (bows) We have come to your summons. How can we be of service?

Magician: Thank you for your alacrity. I am in need of a home, a mansion if you will, where I can practice my trade in comfort, safety, and harmony.

Dwarf Leader: Let us discuss how best we can meet your needs!

Magician: Let us move stage right, gesticulate and discuss and otherwise go over our plans.

Dwarf Leader: I see your gesticulations and divine your mind. BOYS!!

*The Leader turns to the remaining dwarves and snaps his fingers.*

Magician: (aside) The blur of action yon dwarves become as they build the house, furnish it, and put the finishing touches on it is of such rapidity that I myself wonder if Mercury himself might show his quicksilver countenance... Whether to congratulate the work or condemn it as sheer chutzpa I know not.

*Enter Orator.*

Orator: As this house is built the magician furnishes it with rooms, stairs, chairs, and the symbols and associations closest and most important. See, here is a room dedicated to the career and there, a room for hobbies. Over yonder I believe I spy a chapel, or is it a ritual chamber? Beyond that p'raps I divine a great hall for entertaining guests. There really is no limit to what this house might hold and the wise Magician adds to or subtracts from it as necessary. As the outer world changes, so too does the inner home reflect and work with those changes. I believe that the Magician will visit this place often.

*Exit Orator.*

Dwarf Leader: Great Magician, there is one room I would fain show you.

*Dwarf leader opens a great door onto a great library.*

Magician: It is empty but for the finished floors, walls, doors, and windows.

Magician: I smell sawdust.

Dwarf Leader: That is correct! For this room can only be furnished by you.

Magician: Then furnish it I shall. May my wisdom, imagination and intellect be true to the task!

*All Exit.*

## Act II

### Scene 1 – The House

*Enter Orator.*

Orator: This house is the framework that represents the inner self. The Library? Why it represents the magical self. It symbolizes knowledge, experience, and Will!

*Exit Orator.*

*Enter Magician.*

Magician: Argh. My Library. 'Tis undone and needs proper attention. I suppose I've saved the best for last.

*The Magician wanders about, hemming and hawing about how best to furnish the Library.*

*Enter Wise Woman.*

Wise Woman: I thought I would find you here. It's beautiful, you know.

Magician: Er?

Wise Woman: May I have a tour?

Magician: But my Library is unfinished.

Wise Woman: Then take my arm, be a good host and show me 'round. You can save said Library for last!

Magician: Since you put it that way... Allow me!

*Magician takes the Wise Woman on a tour of the house. She comments and compliments and occasionally re-arranges the occasional item and conjures up a gift to augment a particular area. They return to the door of The Library.*

### Scene II – The Library

*Enter Wise Woman and Magician.*

Wise Woman: Ah, we're here.

Wise Woman: This room smells like sawdust.

Magician: I'm a bit embarrassed it's not fin...

Wise Woman: *She whistles sweetly through her fingers.* Yes, it needs a little work.

*Enter several Elves.*

Wise Woman: Allow me to introduce some helpmeets. They can help you properly furnish this Library. Discuss with them how you want your Library to look and feel.

Magician: I think a desk is appropriate.

Elves: *POOF! A Desk appears with a flash.*

Magician: Mmm… how about some books, tapestries and chairs?

Elves: *Poof, Poof, and POOF!*

Magician: Er, I think maybe that should go over there.

*The Elves move some heavy stuff around to soundtrack of assorted grunts, strainings, and testicular swelling hernias.*

Magician: Ah. I believe it is complete. Thank you, Wise Woman, and thank you, kind elves, for your assistance!

*Elves Exit. On stretchers if necessary.*

Wise Woman: Allow me to offer a blessing for this humble home.

> For your home and hearth, I bless this house
> From site to stay,
> From beam to wall,
> From end to end,
> From ridge to basement,
> From balk to roof-tree,
> From found to summit,
> Found and summit.
> (Carmichael, 1900. p. 105)

*Exit Wise Woman.*

Magician: Ah. Now I truly feel at home!

*Exit Magician.*

## Act III – The Tome

### Scene I – The Foyer

*A knock announces a visitor.*

*Enter Magician.*

Magician: I'm coming. Hello! To whom do I have the pleasure of this visit?

*Enter Wizard.*

Wizard: You could have invited me sooner!

Magician: Er?

Wizard: I jest.

Magician: Then, since your mood is jovial, let me give you the two-bit tour.

*Exit Magician and Wizard.*

Scene II – The Library

*Enter Magician and Wizard.*

Magician: And this is my Library.

Wizard: Wonderful. But there is something amiss.

Magician: Oh?

Wizard: One moment while I pace about divining the cause.

Magician: Oh?

Wizard: *Mumbling then:* Aha!

Magician: What?

Wizard: I have it!

Magician: What?!

Wizard: You are missing somewhat.

Magician: What!!?!

Wizard: Come over here to this bookshelf. Do you see this book?

Magician: The impossibly large one that I don't remember placing there?

Wizard: Precisely. It's yours.

Magician: But I thought it was missing.

Wizard: Don't be cheeky.

Magician: Um, what is it?

Wizard: It is your inspiration and guide in difficult times. It is your source of information and wisdom. It provides powerful spells and enchantments to help you achieve your goals. It's your spell book...

but oh so much more!

Magician: As I hold it, it feels... intelligent. But in a passive way.

Wizard: What else?

Magician: I feel that it always opens to the right pages.

Wizard: You are correct. It also has a tendency to glow when it wants your attention. That's its way of letting you know you need a particular piece of information. Even when you don't know you don't need it.

Magician: Splendid. Can I...

Wizard: Yes, you can enter more information into it when you feel so moved. It's a handy tome, that one. Place it there!

*He points to an ornate bookstand that materializes out of thin air.*

Magician: Done.

Wizard: Perfect! Thank you so much for your hospitality. I'll let myself out.

Magician: You are quite...

*Exit Wizard.*

*Fade to Black.*

## Act IV – The Council of The Magi

### Scene I – The Library

*Enter Magician, Wizard, and Wise Woman.*

Magician: It's kind of you to visit me again, but why do you keep giving each other Significant Glances?

Wise Woman: We have somewhat to show you.

Wizard: Follow us.

*They get up and walk to a section of wall in the Library. The wall opens inward into a stone passage way.*

Magician: It's a secret passage!

Wizard: *dryly,* Not anymore.

Magician: Hardeeharharhar.

Wizard: I told you he was cheeky.

Wise Woman: Mmm... Let's go down the passage.

Magician: I do believe this door is locked and must be opened before we can achieve entrance.

Wise Woman: And I do believe this key is for you.

Wizard: It grants you passage to the Council of the Magi.

Magician: Then let's turn the key and be on our way.

*Exit Magician, Wizard, and Wise Woman.*

## Scene II – The Council Chambers of the Magi

*Enter Magician, Wizard and Wise Woman into a vast chamber filled with Various Magical Denizens.*

Magician: This is amazing.

Wizard: Within these chambers you can find a vast array of beings from many planes and places. They come here to discuss their path and offer support, friendship, and advice. In this chamber they all gather as equals.

Wise Woman: You can find quite a bit of support from these folk, but don't phant'sy that the support is always warm and fuzzy. *These* magicians hold you to *their* standards and the constructive criticism they give can vary wildly from visceral and symbolic to rude and uncomfortably blunt.

Magician: I'm getting used to that.

Wise Woman: Cheeky indeed.

Wizard: Remember that these are wise beings and they have a good grasp on how to best help you and support you. In fact, due to that wisdom they may e'en refuse to give you information entirely.

Magician: So it is here I can come to learn how to be a wizard?

Wizard: Aye. By interacting with wizards.

Wise Woman: It is wise to heed the example of a wizard. Come let us introduce you to these magicians, witches, and wizards.

Magician: Those other passageways, do they lead back to their Libraries, Homes and Sacred Spaces?

Wizard: That is likely.

Magician: You don't know?

Wizard: I've only been invited to a few.

Magician: Ah. I take it the keys they carry...

Wise Woman: Serve the same purpose as yours.

*Enter Orator.*

Orator: This small party of folk wanders around the great room for a time. Talking, learning and taking in the sights and wonders of the Council of the Magi.

*Lights begin to dim.*

It's a long and rewarding visit, one that is oft repeated in the future. Fare thee well.

*Fade to black.*

*Finis*

## Mental Association Exercise

This exercise helps teach you to think magically by asking you to think of something as related to, or a part of, other things instead of thinking of it as completely isolated from the world around it. As you work with the exercise you may find that you don't categorize everything explicitly according to the concepts given here. This is acceptable. Applying this in the real world generally means that you use it macrocosmically to consider any object, emotion, experience, or piece of information as a part of a greater whole. This change in perspective alone is powerful.

The exercise utilizes nine concepts, called Paradigms, which highlight the similarities and differences between two ideas. It is very useful for helping you come to terms with the relations between the disparate things you encounter in Reality. Each Paradigm has a title, followed by a definition and an example. Read through all nine concepts and spend a little time thinking about what they mean, how they work, and what kinds of things might fall under each Paradigm. These are derived from Clark (1920).

Collen A'Miketh

## Paradigm One – Inclusion

One idea includes another because it is a general category based on a particular characteristic that the other idea possesses. This relationship can be symbolized by one square within another.

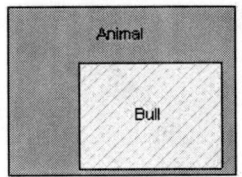 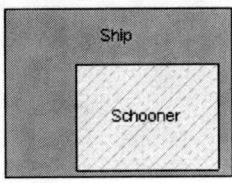 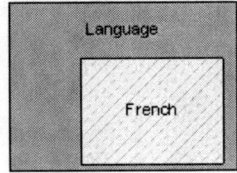

*Examples*
Animal and Cow.
Man and Englishman.
Dwelling and Mansion.

## Paradigm Two – Similarity

Two ideas or objects have something in common or belong to the same class. This relationship is symbolized by squares overlapping.

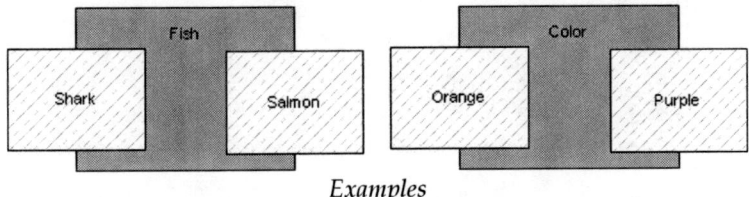

*Examples*

Cow and Horse – Animals.
Chair and Table – Furniture.
Red and Blue – Colors.

## Paradigm Three – Contrast

Two objects or ideas have a characteristic in common but are opposite in degree. Contradiction could be another term used for this association. The relationship of Contrast is illustrated by three squares in contact with each other on the edges.

*Examples*
Heat and Cold are opposite in Temperature;
Youth and Age are opposite ends of Life.
Fire and Water are opposite in Effect.

**Paradigm Four – Partition**

Two things or ideas are respectively whole or part of a common object or definition. At first glance, this has similarities to Paradigm One. However, it differs from the first paradigm in that these two ideas are parts of each other. In Paradigm One, they have something in common. The relation of Partition is shown in the following diagram.

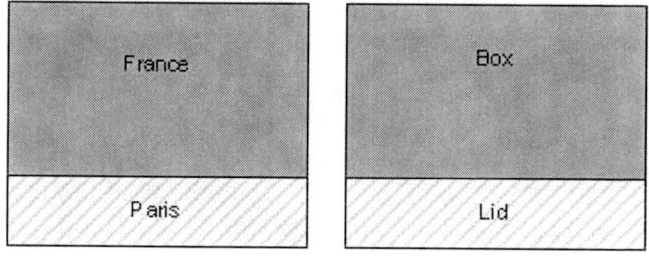

*Examples*
Tree and Branch.
Whale and Blubber.
France and Paris.

**Paradigm Five – Partners**

Two objects or ideas are part of the same thing as a whole. This differs from Paradigm Two because the objects are part of a single unit. In that paradigm the objects are related parts of a uniting idea. The relationship of Partners is shown in the following diagram.

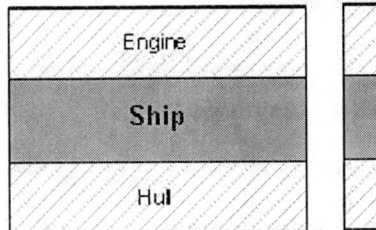 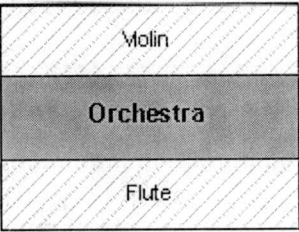

*Examples*
Thumb and Finger are of the hand.
Root and Branch are of the Tree.

## Paradigm Six – Analysis

Two things or ideas are related because one is a property, quality, or descriptor of the other. The following diagram illustrates this relationship.

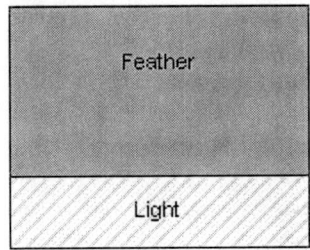 

*Examples*
Lead, Heavy.
Snow, White.
Ball, Round.

## Paradigm Seven – Affinity

Objects are linked together by having a striking quality in common.

*Examples*
Moon, Orange, and Round.

Mountain, Chimney, and High.
Ink, Night, and Black.

### Paradigm Eight – Co-existence

Two objects or ideas associate together in the mind as the result of personal experience, observation, or information.

*Examples*
England, Navy.
Turk, Turban.
China, Wall.
Alaska, Totem.

### Paradigm Nine – Follows

Two ideas are linked together because observation or experience has shown that the second follows the first in time.

*Examples*
Fatigue and Sleep.
Disease and Death.
Gunpowder and Explosion.
Submarine and Sea Disaster.

To utilize this exercise, take an object or idea and map it to each of these nine Paradigms. It may have smaller parts that are related to it, and/or the object may be a piece of a larger whole. For example Moon relates to orange in Paradigm Seven, but could also relate to magic using Paradigm Eight, Round as in Six, Satellite as in Five, The Man in the Moon could tenuously tie to the Moon using Four, The Sun might be considered the Contrast for Paradigm Three, and so on.

Pay particular attention to Paradigm Three - Contrast. It is easy in Western culture to identify something as "opposed" to an idea. It is sometimes difficult to abstract Opposition to the level of Contrast. Example: Good and Evil. Rather than leaving the comparison at opposition, one can Contrast them as opposite ends of an Action or the result of an action. Another example: Positive and Negative are different aspects of Polarity. Hot and Cold are different degrees of temperature.

Collen A'Miketh

## The Phoenix Box Ritual – Long Version

Coming to terms with the filters that box you in is a life long endeavor. The Phoenix Box jumpstarts the process by tackling the box head on and then throwing the limits of your awareness wide open. This ritual takes several days to complete. Read through it once to become familiar with how it should be done before you begin. I have also included a short version to help the time challenged.

Obtain a cardboard box. It can be any size, but preferably no smaller than a shoebox and no larger than two feet on each side (about sixty centimeters).

### Phase 1

Write one word per side on all six sides from the following list: Perception, Awareness, Knowledge, Transformation, Internalization, and Integration. As you write each of these words, imagine that you can only experience these concepts from the *inside* of the box.

### Phase 2

(Phase 2 can be done in tandem with Phase 1 or on a separate occasion.)

Look at the empty inside of the box. Look at the world outside the box. Open both ends and look through the box. Be aware of how the box limits your field of vision. Be aware of how it limits the processes of Perception, Awareness, Knowledge, Transformation, Internalization, and Integration. Set it aside.

### Phase 3

This particular phase is derived from ideas presented by Newman, Berkowitz and Mildred (1986). On another day, meditate on the box again. This time close the bottom of the box so it can hold what you put in it. Look into the box and review your life. Find the one, two, or three incidents in your childhood that defined who you were. See how they define who you are today. Trace how these formative events created a box around your Reality that persists to this day. Place these instances into the box. Put the box aside.

### Phase 4

At another time, come back to the box. Open the box on top and bottom. Cut on its sides and top so it is 6 different parts. Move those parts to the furthest corners of the room you are in. See what the box encompasses. Feel your box of awareness growing and expanding. If possible, take your box to the woods or to a field. Place your six pieces some distance away from you. See what your box encompasses. Place your pieces as far away as you can while still being able to see them. Compare what falls within the field of awareness with this new box. Bring the box back to your altar and place it there for a time.

### Phase 5

When you are ready, burn the box. As it burns, see the flame helping you to integrate your childhood experiences and expand your adult awareness. Feel the shift in your awareness as you open to new possibilities. Once the box is physically gone, make a goal for yourself to always be aware of your new expanded box of awareness and its limits. Make it a point to keep those limits flexible but safe for you. Make it a point to find ways to expand your new box.

## The Phoenix Box Ritual – Short Version

Take the box and beat yourself upon the pate with it while chanting, "Of my limits I am aware. I accept them. I integrate them. I am better person for it."

Allow the thump, thump, thump of the cardboard to penetrate your being.

Do this until you believe it and can honestly and constructively work with who you are.

## The Wizard's Apprentice

Sometimes teaching is the best way to learn. The intent of this exercise is to help you integrate and understand what you have learned by "training" another. This exercise is intended to mimic the teaching process, though I suppose it can be used in the real world as well.

Spend some time thinking about taking an apprentice and what it might entail. Think long and hard on how you will train and instruct this person in what you know and how you do things. *Take your time with this.* Teaching is an awesome responsibility. When you are ready go to your Sacred Space and wait for the apprentice to appear.

Over a period of time, go to your Sacred Space and train

your Apprentice using your own insights and experiences. As you do this, imagine the questions the Apprentice asks, the information the Apprentice challenges, and the difficulties the Apprentice may have. Take notes (yes, that writing thing again) as to how your Apprentice progresses and how you mature by teaching your Apprentice. In fact, you may find yourself doing some very real research in the real world to help answer the questions and difficulties that arise.

Some questions an Apprentice might ask:

What is your personal magical theory?

How does it work?

Why is this the theory you have chosen?

When does it not work?

How does this theory allow you to interact with it?

How does this theory allow for integration?

What is your personal code of conduct?

How do you apply it?

Why do I have to learn this stuff?

What good is it to continue doing this?

Isn't there a better/easier/smarter/cooler/simpler/more cost-effective way?

How does this principle work?

Do I have to perform this spell, ritual, or meditation?

This exercise is difficult, can I skip it? Or, can you help me with it?

Is my insight on this particular lecture ok?

Last, but not least, keep in mind that leading by example is sometimes the best way to teach. No amount of instruction can take the place of this most effective of lessons.

## The Oprah Effect

Alternately, you can imagine yourself on Oprah trying to sell your brand of magic or your answer to Life, the Universe, and whatnot. For a real hoot swap out Oprah for Jerry Springer.

# Chapter Nine: A Miketh's Memoir

In this chapter I present a review of some of the highlights of my career as a magician. And yes, I emphasize the successes and gloss over my spectacular failures. In any event, I hope relaying some of my experiences has some application in your endeavors as a magician.

### My First Spell Ever

Long before I chose to pursue a magical path, at say age ten or eleven, I read a book on witchcraft. It was a historical, if somewhat skewed, account of witchcraft in America and England. I remember bits and pieces of the book itself, mostly the woodcuts, but what I remember more is that I hated my bus driver. So... I decided to curse her. It was a simple affair loosely based on what I had read in the book. Among other things, I remember trying to drink a "potion" of lemonade and chocolate milk... gross. Anyways, after my little curse my bus driver was removed within two weeks.

### Rune Magic

My runic path began when I read Donald Tyson's *Rune Magic* (1988). I was just shy of twenty. I read the book, diddled with the material, and then put it aside. I picked the book up again a couple of years later and spent a couple of months learning the divinatory meanings, fumbling with the rituals and making rune dice. (I still have the dice and use them, too.) Over the next many years, I made a talisman or two and did the odd spell. I did a fair amount of divination. After a couple of backfires and bad experiences, I set them aside again. I was uncomfortable using them. They felt demanding and unhelpful.

Some of my personal pricklies came from my literal interpretation of Tyson's curious ceremonial approach to the subject matter in chapter five. His was the first book I read and had a major impact on my runic interactions whether I wanted it to or not. I finally realized that I strongly disagreed with the "you must protect yourself from the forces of darkness and be spotlessly clean physically, spiritually, and morally" position. To me (and others, if memory serves), we are descendants of Odin and the lawful heirs to runic magic. Odin didn't spend nine days on a world tree so we could be afraid. Respectful, yes. Humble, probably. Prepared, boy howdy that's an affirmative. Afraid? Permission denied. *Any force, good or bad, must come from (or be allowed into) our own mind, heart and life.*

Though I must admit, the runes had become difficult because I hadn't developed a proper relationship with them or their governing deities. To add insult to injury, as a magician I was not mature or experienced and I was too young to have the tools of introspection and humility to work out the issues. I had not acquired the requisite skills of meditation, discipline, and self-realization. I was inclined to approach magic and the runes at face value and I was too literal, too inflexible, and too damned arrogant. Faced with these obstacles, but not really knowing what those obstacles were, I again set the runes aside. One could argue that without the proper skills, setting the runes aside was the wisest thing I could have done.

I didn't officially pick them up again for about five years. I was working with Ogham as part of my Druid training and...well...Ogham just didn't speak to me. So I picked up the runes again. This time, my wife and I went through the material together.

After about six months, I had the meanings memorized and was fairly comfortable with Norse godforms. Working with my wife gave a dimension to my relationship with the runes that I had not had before. I found my own way to use the runes. Instead of strictly Runic spells I used a hybrid of Druid ritual, traditional spells, Celtic and Egyptian godforms, and the Runes. The spells I cast (well, actually "we," as my wife helped with a lot of them) were shockingly effective. Old One Eye hasn't complained, so this hybrid approach is still how I do rune magic.

## My Rune Spell Story

I was working as a network administrator at a bank. I decided to cast a rune spell to get my boss a new job. His job had a Vice President title and it seemed like the most positive way to get some upward mobility for myself. Yeah, I know. The white lies we tell ourselves. Imagine my surprise (and imagine the droll tone I'm using right now) when the runes did not manifest that way at all.

My boss was happy enough in his current position to be "career immobile." This is what happened instead...

A headhunter found an old resume on the 'Net and wanted to talk. He said some things that piqued my curiosity. So I agreed to meet with him. I had a job so it really didn't matter much. I was in it for the free lunch. Long story short, I got the job and turned it down. The headhunters offered more money. I turned it down. They got really pushy and manipulative. I was ill that day and got really cranky (I believe I uttered the phrase "What part of Fuck and You do you not comprehend?") After that pretty little gem of a conversation they offered me a large bonus... I kid you not. *I still said no.* Pushy bastards. They offered me a bigger bonus.

My wife said I was stupid if I didn't take the job. I decided listening to El Presidente was a wise course of action. I said yes. Best job I've ever had. Still working there today. The headhunters don't talk to me anymore. My wife still does.

### Post Script

It's unfortunate that I had to be a penis with ears to get the job. I'm not proud of that. It was out of character and very stressful. Anyways, I think the runes made sure I was where I needed to be to do exactly what I needed to do to get the job that I always wanted. It was one hell of an experience.

### Sigil Magic

I do a fair amount of sigil magic. Sometimes it is bona fide Chaos Sigil Magic and other times I use Norse runes and my own eclectic techniques. In any case, I've had some successes and failures. For shits and grins, I experimented with casting a "win the lottery" sigil. I haven't won the lottery yet, but my luck is improving. I notice that I'm luckier when I have direct line of sight contact with the people who have a bearing on the outcome. This leads me to two observations: First, that many times my luck is dependent on other people and second, making them aware and disposed towards my Will is the key. It also points out to me that Collateral Change happens in spell work, too.

## People Sigil Magic

My formal attempts at PSM have been rather limited. It's almost impossible to do this on myself and there are limited circumstances when my ethical sense of right and wrong permits me to influence other people. They are not just any Joe Shmoe, they are my friends.

One particular attempt stands out. A friend had family difficulties. I spent quite a long time, probably six months or so, thinking about the situation. I weighed, judged, and asked my friend questions, up to and including questions about the possibility of doing some spell work. The situation was complex and I spent a lot of time working through the implications of trying to influence events. There were potential pitfalls for everyone involved (including myself). In the end, I decided to take action.

After I cast my spell(s!) on the Astral, I spent a fair amount of time with my friend. As we discussed the turmoil I sensed myself conveying the reality of my Will to him and taking hold. I was a bit surprised at the sensation, but kept at it. The short-term effects were negligible, but within three months some very surprising changes had taken place. Within a year, things had moved back to where they were before the spell was cast. Some magicians might have felt compelled to try again. They may have been right to do so, but I left things where they were. I had spoken my peace and the final results were not something I had any right to impose my Will upon.

Though the outcome was nebulous, I considered it a success on two levels. The first was the effectiveness of my Astral spellcasting. The second was the effectiveness with which I communicated the spell via non-verbal cues to my friend. Don't ask me what exactly those cues were, or how I gave them. It was a very visceral, borderline surreal, experience that currently defies my ability to explain it.

I also do less formal experiments. I make myself believe a person I care about is a certain way. I sometimes do this with a formal spell, but more often I just actively imagine the person that certain way when I am around them and refuse to accept their version of Reality (if only in my mind...this is a very passive experiment). Healthy, not an alcoholic, losing lots of weight...whatever it is that seems to be something they are struggling with. The results are never immediate, but I consistently observe that within six weeks or so the people start to shape themselves according to the way I see them in my mind. I also notice that there is generally a plateau stage around three months, usually when my attention flags or I don't spend as much time around them, and then it picks up again when I reassert my attention or proximity.

## Astral Plane

The Astral Plane is an amorphous concept for me. I sometimes choose to see it as a product of my mind. At other times I view it as a separate dimension. I suppose that I most often see it as a nexus for potential and don't often question whether that potential comes from me or exists independently. The Astral is a crossroads of awareness, perspective, information, and action coming from or going towards me. I consider it to be my interface between all worlds and Realities.

The Astral is both within me and outside me and represents the three types of Reality I talked about in "It's Just a Theory." This juxtaposition might seem contradictory because I incorporate both the concept that the Astral is fluid and flexible while maintaining that it also encompasses inflexible Reality. This does not seem quite so contradictory when I take into account that the Astral is both what I need, or want, it to be and it can inject its own Reality into my awareness.

## Astral Travel

To travel astrally, while remaining rooted in my body, I make use of bi-location. It is *"a type of Astral projection in which you project yourself astrally while maintaining awareness of everything around you."* (Morphica 2005, *A Witch's Dictionary*.) This is in direct contrast with classic approaches that want me out of my body and on the Astral Plane as some shining being of light. Golden Dawn practices in particular come to mind as examples of this traditional approach. (Regardie, 2001)

Astral Travel relies on an Astral Body. The Astral Body is developed using the Body of Light. Classic interpretations hold said body to be an exact duplicate of my earthly body. This copy contains my emotional and intellectual makeup, but in the form of energy. When I work with classic techniques, I get around the "exact external duplicate" requirement by following the instructions of the classicists while using bi-location.

In other words, I imagine myself on the Astral Plane in spirit form. Then I form an exact duplicate of myself and move my consciousness to it instead of attempting to form the Astral Body in front of my real body sitting in the here and now. I then leave my original Astral Body behind (and by proxy, my real body) and flit about the Astral as a sparkly being hollering "Tink's undies, Rachel!" at anything I encounter. The results are still very effective for me and in accord with my belief that the mind/body are an integrated whole.

### Astral Magic

I have a tendency to do a lot of my Astral work immediately prior to falling asleep. I recall more than one authority recommending against this practice, but my fascination with doing it "the wrong way" stems from an early interest in H.P. Lovecraft's *The Dreamquest for Unknown Kadath*. As a teenager, I liked that story so much that I spent six months trying to cross the threshold into the world of dream. I never did find a physical threshold but, by Cthulhu, I learned to be a lucid dreamer.

In practice, my Astral magic mirrors my real world magic. I perform the same steps in my head that I perform in the flesh. I enter a trance state, perform a ritual, cast a spell and complete the transaction following the same steps I use in the real world. I can do this because I've memorized my rituals, supporting occult material, and symbolism. I favor Astral magic because I can visualize myself as this big badass wizard tossing magic about and instantly molding Reality in ways I see fit.

When I do it too much, though, I find that I develop resistance to the practice, so I balance it with magic in the flesh. I know I've been overdoing it when I find myself unable to meditate or concentrate for any length of time. This invariably prevents me from accomplishing the task at hand. I also find myself getting sidetracked and forgetting to do whatever it is I intend to do.

When I'm not doing Astral magic, I do a bit of meditation just before I fall asleep. Sometimes I go where I intended to go, and sometimes I'm dragged off in another direction. A particularly notable meditation involved receiving a magical tool from my patron goddess and being told it would always manifest my desire. To test this, and in a nod towards Richard Bach, I used the tool to cause a white feather to appear in my waking world.

Within ten days, as I was walking through the parking lot to work, I almost stepped on a white feather. Go figure.

## Bibliomancy

I had one very memorable and quite unexpected experience with bibliomancy. I was studying a historical magical Order. Somewhere in my reading it was stated that no matter where or how a seeker asked, the seeker would get an answer. I decided to test it. Before falling asleep one night, I performed a ritual on the Astral Plane. I journeyed to where I imagined their headquarters would be and left a scroll asking to join. I did not receive an answer that evening. Quite honestly, I didn't expect one.

Later that week, I was repeating a mantra over and over while in light trance. During my exercise, I lost awareness. But when I came back, I realized I was repeating something over and over again. It wasn't the mantra I'd started with. I was repeating over and over, "xxx is the answer." Xxx was a three-digit number. I had no idea what it meant. I took notes in my journal and did a fair amount of research trying to figure out what exactly this answer meant. At that time, I didn't tie it to my little foray asking to join that Order.

A couple of days later, I was working on my "not thinking" skills. Shortly after I reached that state, I received a second three-digit number. I still had no idea what it meant, but figured it was related to my previous experience with the mantra. More research yielded no answer. A day or so later, while not doing anything particularly magical, I realized they were page numbers in a book. I also realized I was pretty sure what book it was. The book was about the Order I had been researching. I went home that evening and looked up both pages. The first number took me to a page that was clearly intended as proof that the message was for me and the second number took me to a page that said, effectively, "Don't call us, we'll call you."

Though I was turned down, I was quite excited at having had this experience.

## Weather Control

Just kidding. I use my thermostat.

# Bibliography

Agrippa, H. C. (1651). What Magic Is, What Are the Parts Thereof, and How the Professors Thereof Must Be Qualified. In H.C. Agrippa, *Three Books of Occult Philosophy* (p. 41). London: R.W. for Gregory Moule.

Bardon, F. (2007). Magical Schooling of the Spirit. In F. Bardon, *Initiation Into Hermetics* (p. 97). Salt Lake City: Merkur Publishing Company.

Bellows, H. A. (1936). *The Poetic Edda, Sigdrifumol.* Retrieved April 2, 2008, from Internet Sacred Text Archive: http://www.sacred-texts.com/nue/poe/poe25.htm

Black, J. A., Fluckiger-Hawker, E., Robson, E., & Zolyomi, G. (1998). *The Electronic Corpus of Sumerian Literature.* Retrieved January 30, 2008, from Oxford University: http://etcs1.orinst.ox.ac.uk/section1/tr141.htm. (Lines 164 to 172.)

Carmichal, A. (1900). *Carmina Gadelica, Volume I.* Retrieved January 30, 2008, from Internet Sacred Text Archive: http://www.sacred-texts.com/neu/celt/cg1/cg1048.htm

Carroll, P. J. (1987). Liber MMM. In P.J. Carroll *Liber Null and Psychonaut.* (pp. 16-18 and p.22) Boston: Red Wheel/Weiser, LLC.

Carroll, P. J. (1992). Yellow Magic. In P.J. Carroll *Liber Kaos.* (pp. 122-128) Boston: Red Wheel/Weiser, LLC.

Clark, W. (circa 1920). *Power and Force.* Philadelphia: John C. Winston Publishing. The only known originals are currently in my private collection. The story about how I came across them is a good one. Buy me a beer and I'll tell it to you. Buy yourself a couple three beers and you might actually enjoy it.

Crowley, A. (2004). Pranayama and its Parallel in Speech, Mantrayoga. In A. Crowley, *Book 4* (pp. 18-21). Boston: Red Wheel/Weiser, LLC.

Hall, M. P. (2003). The Ancient Mysteries and Secret Societies. In M. P. Hall, *The Secret Teachings of All Ages* (pp. 39-78). New York: Penguin.

Hine, P. (1995). *Condensed Chaos.* Tempe, AZ: New Falcon Publications.

King, J. (1999). The Agricultural Cycle and The Annual Ceremonies. In J. King, *The Celtic Druids' Year* (pp. 106-140). London: Blandford Press.

Leadbeater, C. W. (1998). *Freemasonry and its Ancient Mystic Rites.* New York: Gramercy Books.

Levi, E. (1922). Magic and Magism. In E. Levi, *The Paradoxes of the Highest Science.* Retrieved January, 30th, 2008 from Internet Sacred Text Archive: http://www.sacred-texts.com/eso/levi/phs/phs11.htm. (p. 98) Calcutta: Calcutta Central Press Co.

Levi, E. (1922). Knowledge is the Ignorance or Negation of Evil. In E. Levi, *The Paradoxes of the Highest Science.* Retrieved January, 30th, 2008 from Internet Sacred Text Archive: http://www.sacred-texts.com/eso/levi/phs/phs07.htm. (p. 45). Calcutta: Calcutta Central Press Co.

Levi, E. (1974). The Religion of Magic. In E. Levi, & A. E. Waite (Ed.). *The Mysteries of Magic.* (p. 383). New Jersey: University Books, Inc. The original quote is "*Faith is superstition and madness if reason be not at its foundation.*"

Levi, E. (1974). The Threshold of Magical Science. In E. Levi, & A. E. Waite (Ed.). *The Mysteries of Magic.* (pp. 49-50). New Jersey: University Books, Inc.

Liminality. (2008, March). In *Wikipedia, the free encyclopedia.* Retrieved March 22, 2008, from http://en.wikipedia.org/wiki/liminality

McCoy, E. (1995). The Celtic Pantheon and the Wheel of the Year. In E. McCoy, *Celtic Myth and Magic* (pp. 81-96). St. Paul: Llewellyn Publications.

Morphica. (2005). *A Witch's Dictionary.* Retrieved March 25, 2008, from Blog Drive: http://ggbasics.blogdrive.com

Newman, M., Berkowitz, B., & Owen, J. (1986). *How To Be Your Own Best Friend.* New York: Ballantine Books.

Newton's Laws of Motion. (2008, September). In *Wikipedia, the free encyclopedia.* Retrieved September 7, 2008 from http://en.wikipedia.org/wiki/Newton%27s_laws_of_motion

Pennick, N. (1998). Making Talismans. In N. Pennick, *Secrets of the Runes* (pp. 172-176). London: Thorsons.

Regardie, I. (2001). The Training of the Will. In I. Regardie, *The Tree of Life* (p. 191). St. Paul: Llewellyn Publications.

Regardie, I. (2001). Magical Correspondences, Tools, and Techniques. In I. Regardie, *The Tree of Life* (pp. 172-175). St. Paul: Llewellyn Publications.

Regardie, I. (2001). Skrying and Astral Projection. In I. Regardie, *The Tree of Life* (pp. 221-262). St. Paul: Llewellyn Publications.

Sri Sathya Sai Baba. (n.d.). Retrieved January 30th, 2008 from thinkexist.com: http://thinkexist.com/quotation/before-you-speak-think-is-it-necessary-is-it-true/350699.html.

St. Ignatius of Loyola (circa 1522). In Mottala, A. (1964). *The Spiritual Exercises of St. Ignatius*. New York: Doubleday.

Three Initiates. (1912). The Principle of Vibration. In *The Kybalion* (p. 10). Chicago: Yogi Publication Society.

Tyson, D. (1988). *Rune Magic*. St. Paul: Llewellyn Publications.

# Did You Like What You Read?

*Mastering the Art of Ritual Magick, Volume One* by Frater Barrabbas
978-1-905713-21-9/MB0121
$21.99/£12.99 paperback
The first in a three-volume set which serves to demystify the practice of ritual magick and promote a personal magickal regimen.

*The Paradigmal Pirate* by Joshua Wetzel
ISBN 1-905713-00-2/MB0100
$21.99/£12.99 paperback
A grimoire of practical magical training with ritual work and useful methodologies and rituals for effecting change with the techniques of chaos magic..

*The Pop Culture Grimoire* edited by Taylor Ellwood
ISBN 978-1-905713-22-6 / MB0123
$20.99/£12.99 paperback
This new anthology covers never-before-seen techniques for incorporating the entities, images, and themes from pop culture, developed by magicians such as Lisa McSherry, Andrieh Vitimus, and Lupa.

*The Magician's Reflection* by Bill Whitcomb
ISBN 978-1-905713-23-3 / MB0124
$21.99/£12.99 paperback
Long out of print, this essential guide to magical symbols, archetypes, and their use is available in a new, revised edition. Don't just settle for someone else's sacred signs—create your own!

## Find these and the rest of our current lineup at http://www.immanion-press.com

Printed in the United States
143052LV00002B/11/P